CRACK'D
POT
TRAIL

Also by Steven Erikson

STEVEN ERIKSON

CRACK'D

POT

TRAIL

A Malazan Tale of Bauchelain and Korbal Broach

TOR®

A TOM DOHERTY ASSOCIATES BOOK

NEW YORK

CRACK'D POT TRAIL

Copyright © 2009 by Steven Erikson

A Tor Book
Published by Tom Doherty Associates, LLC
175 Fifth Avenue
New York, NY 10010

www.tor-forge.com

Tor® is a registered trademark of Tom Doherty Associates, LLC.

Library of Congress Cataloging-in-Publication Data

Erikson, Steven.
    Crack'd pot trail : a malazan tale of Bauchelain and Korbal Broach /
Steven Erikson.—1st U.S. ed.
        p. cm.
    "A Tom Doherty Associates book."
    ISBN 978-0-7653-3046-8 (hardcover)
    ISBN 978-0-7653-2425-2 (trade paperback)
    I. Title.
    PR9199.4.E745C73 2011
    813'.6—dc22   2011018992

First published in Great Britain by PS Publishing Ltd. by arrangement with the author

First U.S. Edition: September 2011

Printed in the United States of America

0 9 8 7 6 5 4 3 2 1

CRACK'D POT TRAIL

"There will always be innocent victims in the pursuit of evil."

The long years are behind me now. In fact, I have never been older. It comes to a man's career when all of his cautions—all that he has held close and private for fear of damaging his reputation and his ambitions for advancement—all in a single moment lose their constraint. The moment I speak of, one might surmise, arrives the day—or more accurately, the first chime after midnight—when one realizes that further advancement is impossible. Indeed, that caution never did a thing to augment success, because success never came to pass. Resolved I may be that mine was a life gustily pursued, riches admirably attained and so forth, but the resolution is a murky one nonetheless. Failure wears many guises, and I have worn them all.

The sun's gilded gift enlivens this airy repose, as I sit, an old man smelling of oil and ink, scratching with this worn quill whilst the garden whispers on all sides and the nightingales crouch mute on fruit-heavy branches. Oh, have I waited too long? Bones ache, twinges abound, my wives eye me from the shadows of the colonnade with black-tipped tongues poking out from painted mouth, and in the adjudicator's office the water-clock dollops measured patience like the smacking of lips.

Well I recall the glories of the holy cities, when in disguise I knelt before veiled tyrants and god-kissed mendicants of the soul, and in the deserts beyond the crowded streets the leather-faced wanderers of the caravan tracks draw to the day's end and the Gilk guards gather in shady oases and many a time I traveled among them, the adventurer none knew, the poet with the sharp eyes who earned his keep unraveling a thousand tales of ancient days—and days not so ancient, if only they knew.

They withheld nothing, my rapt listeners, for dwelling in a desert makes a man or woman a willing audience to all things be they natural or unnatural; while I, for all the wounds I delivered, for all the words of weeping and the joys and all the sorrows of love and death that passed my tongue, smooth as olives, sweetly grating as figs, I never let a single drop of blood. And the night would draw on, in laughter and tears and expostulations and fervent prayers for forgiveness (eyes ashine from my languid explorations of the paramour, the silk-drenched beds and the flash of full thigh and bosom) as if the spirits of the sand and the gods of the whirlwinds might flutter in shame and breathless shock—oh no, my friends, see them twist in envy!

My tales, let it be known, sweep the breadth of the world. I have sat with the Toblai in their mountain fastnesses, with the snows drifting to bury the peeks of the longhouses. I have stood on the high broken shores of the Perish, watching as a floundering ship struggled to reach shelter. I have walked the streets of Malaz City, beneath Mock's brooding shadow, and set eyes upon the Deadhouse itself. Years alone assail a mortal wanderer, for the world is round and to witness it all is to journey without end.

But now see me in this refuge, cooled by the trickling fountain, and the tales I recount upon these crackling sheets of papyrus, they are the heavy fruits awaiting the weary traveler in yonder oasis. Feed then or perish. Life is but a search for gardens and gentle refuge, and here I sit waging the sweetest war, for I shall not die while a single tale remains to be told. Even the gods must wait spellbound.

Listen then, nightingale, and hold close and sure to your branch. Darkness abides. I am but a chronicler, occasional witness and teller of magical lies in which hide the purest truths. Heed me well, for in this particular tale I have my own memory, a garden riotous and overgrown yet, dare I be so bold, rich in its fecundity, from which I now spit these gleaming seeds. This is a story of the Nehemoth, and of their stern hunters, and too it is a tale of pilgrims and poets, and of me, Avas Didion Flicker, witness to it all.

There on the pilgrim route across the Great Dry, twenty-two days and twenty-three nights in a true season from the Gates of Nowhere to the Shrine of the Indifferent God, the pilgrim route known to all as Cracked Pot Trail. We begin with the wonder of chance that should gather in one place and at one time such a host of travelers, twenty-three days beyond the Gate. And too the curse of mischance, that the season was unruly and not at all true.

Across the bleak wastes the wells were dry, the springs mired in foul mud. The camps of the Finders were abandoned, their hearth-ashes cold. Our twenty-third day, yet we still had far to go.

Chance for this gathering. Mischance for the straits these travelers now found themselves in. And the tale begins on this night, in a circle round a fire.

What is a circle but the mapping of each and every soul?

The Travellers Are Described

In this circle let us meet Mister Must Ambertroshin, doctor, footman and carriage driver to the Dantoc Calmpositis. Broad of shoulder and once, perhaps, a soldier in a string of wars, but for him the knots have long since been plucked loose. His face is scarred and seamed, his beard a nest of copper and iron. He serves the elderly woman who never leaves the tall carriage, whose face is ever hidden behind the heavy curtains of the windows. As with others here, the Dantoc is on pilgrimage. Wealth yields little succour when the soul spends too freely, and now she would come bowl in hand to beg before the Indifferent God. On this night and for them both, however, benediction is so distant it could well be on the other side of the world.

Mister Must is of that amiable type, a walking satchel of small skills, quick to light his pipe in grave consideration. Each word he speaks is measured as a miser's coin, snapping sharp upon the wooden tabletop so that one counts by sound alone even when numbers are of no interest. By his singular squint people listen to him, suspicious perhaps of his cleverness, his wise secrets. Whiskered and solid, he is everyman's footman, and many fates shall ride upon his shoulders anon.

The second circle is a jostled one, a detail requiring some explanation. There are two knights among the Nehemothanai, the stern pursuers of the most infamous dread murderers and conjurers Bauchelain and Korbal Broach, and close upon the corpse-strewn trail of these two blackguards are these dangerous men and women, perhaps only days from their quarry. But there is more to their urgency. It is said a mysterious woman leads a vengeful army, also seeking the heads of Bauchelain and Korbal Broach. Where is she? None here know.

Tulgord Vise has announced himself the Mortal Sword of the Sisters, and he is purity in all but name. His cloak is lined in white fur downy as a maiden's scented garden. The bold enameled helm covering his stentorian skull gleams like egg-white on a skillet. His coat of polished mail smiles in rippling rows of silver teeth. The pommel of his proud sword is an opal stone any woman could not help but reach out and touch—were she so brave, so bold.

His visage glows with revelation, his eyes are the nuggets of a man with a secret hoard none could hope to find. All evil he has

seen has died by his hand. All nobility he has granted by his presence he has sired in nine months' time. This is Tulgord Vise,
knight and champion of truth in the holy light of the Sisters.

Wheel now to the other knight, so brash as to intrude upon the
Mortal Sword's winsome claim to singular piety. By title, Arpo
Relent is a Well Knight, hailing from a distant city that once was
pure and true but now, by the bone-knuckled hands of Bauchelain and Korbal Broach, a sunken travesty of all that it had once
been. So does the Well Knight charge, and so too is announced
the very heart of his vow of vengeance.

If blessed white bolsters the mien of Tulgord Vise, it is the gold
of the sun to gilt Arpo Relent's stolid intransigence and the con-
catenation of comportment between these two knights promise a
most uncivil clash to come. Arpo is broad of chest. Sibling swords,
long-bladed and scabbarded in black wood filigreed in gold, are
mounted one upon each hip, with pommels like golden eggs that
could hatch a woman's sigh, and proud indeed of these weapons
is Arpo Relent, and most unmindful of sighs is this paragon of
chastity, and what might we make of that?

With the company of three brothers who might well beat up goril-
las for merriment, Relish Chanter could be destined to live a life
unplucked, and had not Tiny Chanter himself stared hard at the
haggle of artists and said, clear as the chop of an axe, that any
man who deflowered sweet Relish would get cut so clean not even
a starving sparrow could find the worm?

In the middle of this stark, blood-draining pronouncement

from her biggest brother, Relish had wandered off. She'd heard it a thousand times, after all. But what is known at present and what is to become known are different things. For now, let us look upon this most charmingly witless woman.

Black silk, as all know, is the mourner's vanity, and one is reminded of such flowing tresses when looking upon Relish's hair, and in the frame of such dangerous honey there resides a round face with cheeks blushed like slapped buttocks, and raven feathered lashes slyly offering obsidian eyes to any who would seek to claim them. Fullest of bosom and pouched below the arms, sweetly round of belly and broad-hipped, this description alas betrays a sultry confession, as I am yet to note clothing of any sort.

But such brothers! Tiny's mother, lost in the forest of Stratem beneath a most terrible storm, found refuge in a cavern, plunging straight into the arms of a cave bear, but in the instant of crushing contact, all notions of culinary anticipation alighting fires in the bear's brain quickly vanished and in their place a sudden expostulation of amorous possibility lifted them both heavenward. Who would knuckle brow at the audacity of such claims, when the offspring of the wrestlers' pact stood solid and true before all witnesses? The giant man's eyes dispensed all confusion regarding the contrariness of his name, for they were beastly small and rimmed in lurid red with all manner of leakage milking the corners. His nose was a snubbed snout glistening at the scent of blood. His teeth had the busyness of rodents. He bore the muscles of three men misaligned upon his ursine frame and hair sprouted from unlikely places to match the unlikely cunning of the words trickled out from between curling lips.

His brothers held him in much terror, but in this detail's veracity one must roll in a bed of salt given the malice of their regards upon the turn of Tiny's montane back. Midge Chanter was twin to Flea Chanter, both being the get of their mother's misadventures upon a sea strand where walruses warred in the mating season and she had the tusk-gouged scars to prove it. Such origins are beyond argument, lest whiskers twitch and malodorous weights heave upward and close in deadly lunge. Unlike Tiny and his beastly cloak, Midge and Flea wore with brazen pride the hides of their forbearer.

Other siblings abound, t'was said, but mercy held them at bay with a beater's stick, elsewhere and of their grim tale we must await some other night here at the flames of poetic demise.

Among the circle of hardened hunters but one remains. Silent as a forest and professional as a yeoman, Steck Marynd is no boister of past deeds. Mysteries hide in the crooks of roots, and if eyes glitter from the holes of knots their touch is less than a whisper upon death's own shadow. He is nothing but the man seated before us. His face is flat, his eyes are shallow, his lips thin and his mouth devoid of all depth. His beard is black but sparse, his ears small as an ape's and muscled as a mule's as they independently twitch at every whisper and scuff. He chews his words into leather strips that slap wetly at night and dry up like eels in the day's sun.

Upon the back of his shaggy horse he carries a garrison's arsenal, each weapon plain but meticulously clean and oiled. He has journeyed half the world upon the trail of the Nehemoth, yet of the crime to spur such zeal he will say nothing.

We now turn, with some relief, to the true pilgrims and of these there are three distinct groups, each group seeking blessing at a different altar (though in truth and as shall be seen, they are all one and the same). Sages, priests and scholars stiffen their collars to unwelcome contradictions that nevertheless speak true, but as I am none of these worthies, uncollared as it were, that which on the surface makes no sense disturbs me not. Thus, we have a host of parallel tracks all destined to converge.

The Dantoc Calmpositis, eldest among the venerable Dantocs of Reliant City, must remain a creature unknown. Suffice it to say she was the first to set out from the Gates of Nowhere and her manservant Mister Must Ambertroshin, seated on the high bench of the carriage, his face shielded by a broad woven hat, uttered his welcome to the other travelers with a thick-volumed nod, and in this generous instant the conveyance and the old woman presumed within it became an island on wheels round which the others clustered like shrikes and gulls, for as everyone knows, no island truly stays in one place. As it crouches upon the sea and sand so too it floats in the mind, as a memory, a dream. We are cast out from it and we yearn to return. The world has run aground, history is a storm, and like the Dantoc Calmpositis, we would all *hide in anonymity among the fragrant flowers and virtuous nuts, precious to none and a stranger to all.*

Among the pilgrims seeking the shrine of the Indifferent God is a tall hawk of a man who was quick to offer his name and each time he did so an expectant look came to his vultured eyes, for did we not know him? Twitches would find his narrow face in the roaring blankness of our ignorance, and if oil glistened on and dripped from the raven feathered hair draped down the sides of his pressed-in head, well, none of us would dare comment, would we? But this man noted all and scratched and pecked his list of offenders and in the jerking bobs of his rather tiny head anyone near would hear a grackling sound commensurate with the duly irritated; and off he would march, destination certain but unknown, in the manner of a cock exploring an abandoned henhouse.

Well attired and possibly famous and so well comforted by material riches that he could discard them all (for a short time, at least), he proclaimed for himself the task of host among the travelers, taking a proprietary air in the settling of camp at day's end beginning on that first night from the Gates of Nowhere, upon finding the oddly vacated Finder habitations past the old tumulus. He would, in the days and nights to come, grasp hold of this role even as his fine coat flew to tatters and swirling feathers waked his every step, and the cockerel eye-glint would sharpen its madness as the impossible solitude persisted.

Clearly, he was a man of sparrow fates. Yet in the interest of fairness, our host was also a man of hidden wounds. Of that I am reasonably certain, and if he knew wealth so too he had once known destitution, and if anonymity now haunted him, once there had roosted infamy. Or at least notoriety.

Oh, and his name, lest we forget, was Sardic Thew.

Seeking the shrine of an altogether different Indifferent God, we come at last to the poets and bards. Ahead, in the city of Farrog, waited the Festival of Flowers and Sunny Days, a grand fete that culminated in a contest of poetry and song to award one supremely talented artist the Mantle proclaiming him or her The Century's Greatest Artist. That this is an annual award, one might hesitantly submit, simply underscores the fickle nature of critics and humans alike.

The world of the artist is a warrened maze of weasels, to be sure. Long bodies of black fur snake underfoot, quick to nip and snick. One must dance for fame, one must pull up skirts or wing out carrots for an instant's shudder of validation or one more day's respite from the gnawing world. Beneath the delighted smiles and happy nods and clasped forearms and whatnot, resides the grisly truth that there is no audience grand and vast enough to devour them all. No, goes the scurrilous conviction, the audience is in fact made up of five people, four of whom the artist knows well and in so knowing trusts not a single utterance of opinion. And who, pray tell, is that fifth person? That stranger? That arbiter of omnipotent power? No one knows. It is torture.

But one thing is certain. Too many artists for one person. Therefore, every poet and every painter and every bard and every sculptor dreams of murder. Just to snap hand downward, grasp hard the squirming snarling thing, and set it among one's foes!

In this respect, the artists so gathered in this fell group of travelers, found in the truth to come an answer to their most fervent prayers. Pity them all.

But enough commiseration. The poet has made the nest and must squat in it whilst the vermin seethe and swarm up the crack of doubt and into fickle talent's crotch. Look then, upon Calap Roud, the elder statesman of Reliant City's rotundary of artists, each of whom sits perched in precarious perfection well above the guano floor of the cage (oh of course it is gilded). This is Calap's twenty-third journey across the Great Dry of inspiration's perdition, and he is yet to win the Mantle.

Indeed, in his wretchedly long life, he draws close upon the century himself. One might even claim that Calap Roud is the Mantle, though none might leap for joy at the prospect of taking him home, even for a fortnight. There is a miserable collection of alchemies available to the wealthy and desperate (and how often do those two thrash limbs entwined in the same rickety bed?) to beat off the three cackling crows of old age, death, and ambition's dusty bowl, and Calap Roud remains a sponge of hope, smelling of almonds and cloves and lizard gall-bladders.

And so with the miracle of elixirs and a disgustingly strong constitution, Calap Roud looks half his age, except for the bitter fury in his eyes. He waits to be discovered (for even in Reliant City his reputation was not one of discovery but of pathetic bullying, backstabbing, sordid underhand graft and of course gaggles of hangers-on of all sexes willing, at least on the surface, to suffer the wriggle of Calap's fickler every now and then; and worse of all, poor Calap knows it's all a fraud). Thus, whilst he has stolen a thousand sonnets, scores of epic poems and millions of clever offhanded comments uttered by talented upstarts stupidly within range of his hearing, at his very core he stares, mouth open, upon a chasm on all sides, wind howling and buffeting him as he totters on his perch. Where is the golden cage? Where are all the white-headed fools he shat upon? There's nothing down there but more down there going so far down there is no there at all.

Calap Roud has spent his entire albeit modest fortune bribing every judge he could find in Farrog. This was his last chance. He would win the Mantle. He deserved it. Not a single one of the countless vices hunting the weakling artists of the world dragged him down—no, he had slipped free of them all on a blinding road of virtuous living. He was ninety-two years old and this year, he would be discovered!

No alchemies or potions in the world could do much about the fact that, as one grew older and yet older, so too one's ears and nose. Calap Roud, as modestly wrinkled as a man in his late forties, had the ears of a veteran rock ape of G'danisban's coliseum and the nose of a probiscus monkey who'd instigated too many tavern brawls. His teeth were so worn down one was reminded of catfish mouths biting at nipples. From his old man's eyes came a leer for every woman, and from his leer came out a worm-like tongue with a head of purple veins.

Object of his lust, more often than not, was to be found in the Nemil beauty sitting languidly upon the other side of the fire (and if temptation burns where else would she be?). Purse Snippet was a dancer and orator famous across the breadth of Seven Cities. Need it be even said that such a combination of talents was sure to launch spurting enthusiasm among the heavy-breathing multitudes known to inhabit cities, towns, villages, hamlets, huts, caves and closets the world over?

Lithe was her smile, warm her midnight hair, supple of tongue her every curvaceous utterance, Purse Snippet was desired by a thousand governors and ten thousand nobles. She had been offered palaces, islands in artificial lakes, entire cities. She had been offered a hundred slaves each trained in the arts of love, to serve her pleasure until age and jealous gods took pleasure away. Lavished with jewels enough to adorn a hundred selfish queens in their dark tombs. Sculptors struggled to render her likeness in marble and bronze, and then committed suicide. Poets fell so far inside their poems of adoration and worship they forgot to eat and died at their garrets. Great warleaders tripped and impaled themselves on their own swords in pursuit of her. Priests foreswore drink and children. Married men surrendered all caution in their secret escapades. Married women delighted in exposing and then murdering their husbands with ridicule and savage exposes.

And none of it was enough to soothe the unreasoning fires crisping black her soul. Purse Snippet knew she was the Thief of Reason. She stole wisdom from the wise and made them fools, but all that she took simply slid like lead dust between her amorously perfected fingers. She was also the Thief of Desire, and lust pursued her like a tidal surge and where it passed other women were left bloodless and lifeless. But with her own desires she was lost in frantic search, unable to alight long on any branch, no matter how inviting it had at first seemed.

So she had found a grey powder that she took in draughts of wine and this powder which had so blissfully taken her away from everything now revealed its true self. It was the Thief of her Freedom.

She would enter the famous shrine of the Indifferent God, seeking the blessing that none other had ever achieved. She believed she could win this, for she intended to dance and sing as she had never before danced and sang. She would steal the indifference from a god. She would.

She could not remember when last she had felt free, but she could not think of anything she wanted more.

Each night, alas, the powder beckoned her.

Arch rival to Calap Roud was the illimitable, ambitious, inexcusably young Brash Phluster. That he delighted in the old bastard's presence on this journey could hardly be refuted, for Brash so wanted Calap to witness youth's triumph in Farrog. With luck, it would kill him.

Seven years Calap had been defecating on Brash, trying to keep him down on the crusty floor, but Brash was not one to let a rain of guano discourage his destiny. He knew he was brilliant in most things, and where he lacked brilliance he could fill those spaces with bold bluster and entirely unfounded arrogance. A sneer was as good as an answer. A writhe of the lip could slice throats across the room. He eyed Calap as would a wolf eye a dog, appalled at a shared pedigree and determined to tear the sad thing to pieces at the first opportunity.

True talent was found in the successful disguise of genius, and Brash accounted himself a master of disguises. His future was glory, but he would reveal not a single hint, not one that some cragged critic or presumptuous rival might close in on, stoat fangs bared. No, they could dismiss him each and every day for the time being. He would unveil himself in Farrog, and then they would all see. Calap Roud, that stunning watery-eyed dancer, Purse Snippet, and the Entourage too—

The Entourage! Whence comes such creatures so eager to abandon all pretense of the sedentary? One envisages haste of blubbering excitement, slippery gleam in the eye, a lapdog's brainless zeal, as a canvas bag is stuffed full of slips and whatnot, with all the grace of a fakir backstage moments before performing before a gouty king. A whirlwind rush through rooms like shrines, and then out!

Pattering feet, a trio, all converging in unsightly gallop quick to feminize into a skip and prance once He Who Is Worshipped is in sight. The Entourage accompanies the Perfect Artist everywhere, gatherings great and small, public and intimate. They build the walls of the formidable, impregnable keep that is the Perfect Artist's ego. They patrol the moat, flinging away all but the sweetest defecatory intimations of mortality. They stand sentinel in every postern gate, they gush down every sluice, they are the *stained glass to paint rainbows upon their beloved's perfectly turned profile.*

But let us not snick and snack overmuch, for each life is a wonder unto itself, and neither contempt nor pity do a soul sound measures of health, lest some issue of envy squeeze free in unexpectedly public revelation. The object of this breathless admiration must wait for each sweet woman's moment upon the stage in the bull's eye lantern light of our examination.

To begin, we shall name all three and attach to each select obtuberances in aid of future recollection. Sellup, first for no particular reason, has seen twenty-three summers and remembers in excruciating detail four of them, from the moment she first set eyes upon her beloved Perfect Artist to the very present found in this tale. Of her first eighteen years she has no memory whatsoever. Was she born? Did she possess parents? Did they love her? She cannot recall. Brothers? Sisters? Lovers? Offspring? Did she eat? Did she sleep?

Dark brown and springy was her hair, whirling in spirals down upon her shoulders. Singular was her eyebrow yet miraculously independent in its expressions at each end. Her nose, narrow and jutting, bore all the mars of inveterate ill-considered interjection. Her mouth cannot be described for it never ceased moving long enough for an accurate appraisal, but her chin jutted with blurred assurance. Of her body beneath her flowery attire, no knowledge is at hand. Suffice it to say she sat a saddle well with nary a pinch upon the horse's waist. Sellup of the blurred mouth, then.

Next was Pampera, linguistically challenged in all languages including her native one, hers was the art of simpering, performed in a serried host of mannerisms and transitory parades from pose to pose, each pose held, alas, both an instant too long and never long enough. In the span of one's self settling into a chair, Pampera could promenade from crosslegged on a silk cushion with elbows upon inside knees and long fingers laced to bridge the weight of her chin (and presumably all the rest above it) to a sudden languorous stretching of one long perfectly moulded leg, flinging back her head with arms rising in rampant stretch to lift and define her savage breasts, before rising to her feet like smoke, swinging round with a pivot of her fine hips wheeling into view the barrel cask of her buttocks before pitching down on the divan, hair flowing like tentacles as she propped up her head with one hand whilst the other (hand, not head) endeavoured to reinsert her breasts into the skimpy cups the style and size of which she likely settled upon a month into puberty.

For Pampera, it must be noted, puberty was buried beneath virginity deep in a tomb long sealed by a thick mound of backfill, with the grass growing thick and high and all significance of the hump long lost to the memory of the local herders. Despite this, she was nineteen years old. Her hair, for all its tidal pool titillations, was the hue of honey though tipped with black kohl ink a finger's width at the ends. She had the eyes of a boy's fantasy, when eyes meant something, the two of them being overlarge and balanced just so to hint at warm scented boudoirs wherein things slid from mothering to something other with all the ease of a blinking lid (or two). Sculptors might dream of smoothing out her likeness in golden wax or creamy clay. Painters might long to lash her fineness to canvas or stuccoed wall, if not ceiling. But one could not but suspect the obsession was doomed to be short lived. Can an object of lust prove much too lust-worthy? Just how many *poses are possible in the world and how did she come by them all? Why, even in sleep her repose palpitates in propitious perfection. The sculptor, looking upon this, would despair to discover that Pampera is her own sculpture and there was naught to be done to match or hope to improve upon it. Painters might fall into toxic madness seeking to match the tone of her flawless skin and it is to the toxic we will return to precipitate our reminding of dearest Pampera.*

Could a poet hope to match her essence in words without an intermission of nausea?

To return to these three, then, we at last come to Oggle Gush, innocent of all depravity not through inexperience, but through blissful imperviousness to all notions of immorality. A slip of mere sixteen years since the day in wonder her mother issued her forth, as naturally unaware of her pregnancy as she was of the innocence her daughter would so immaculately inherit, Oggle Gush deserves nothing but forgiving accolades from paladins and scoundrels alike (excepting only Great Artists). Ever quick to smile even at the most inappropriate of times, shying like a pup from a master's twitching boot one moment only to cuddle in his lap upon the next, squirming as only a thing of claws, wet nose and knobby limbs can.

Not one of her deeds was ill-meant. Not one of the numerous fatal accidents trailing her could be set upon her threshold. When she sang, as she often did, she could not find a solid key if it was glued to her tongue, but all looked on in damp-eyed adoration—and what, perchance, were all thinking? Was this an echo of personal conceits crushed and abandoned in childhood? Was it the unblinking boldness of the talentless that triggered reminiscences of childish lavishments? Or was it something in her dramatic earnestness that disengaged some critical faculty of the brain, leaving only sweet-smelling mush?

Oggle Gush, child of wonder and plaything of the Great Artist, all memory of you is sure to remain immortal and unchanging. As pure as nostalgia, and the cold cruelty with which you were misused, ah, but does this not take us to the Great Artist himself, he with the Entourage? But it does indeed.

Nifty Gum has thrice won the Mantle of the Century's Greatest Artist. His Entourage of three as found upon the trail across the Great Dry, only a month past numbered six hundred and fifty-four, and if not for Oggle's well-intentioned housecleaning beneath the deck of the transport barge, why, they'd all still be with him. As if Oggle knew a thing about boats and whatnot. As if she even understood the function of hull plugs and drain holes, or whatever those things were called.

He looked taller than he looked, if one can say such a thing and by the sure nods all round, it seems that one can. He wore his cloak and measured his stride as if he was a bigger man than he was, and not one of his even features could be said to be exaggerated yet neither were they refined. In gathered host they were pleasant on his face, but should one find them neatly severed and arrayed among rivals on a hawker's bazaar table, why, none would *even so much as reach for them, much less buy them—except, perhaps, as curios of mundanity.*

Of talent's measure Nifty Gum had an ample helping, nothing to overflow the brim, yet something, a fire, a wink, a perspicacity for promotion, the brazen swanning of his sweep and flurry in passage (trailed as ever by his giggling entourage), something or perhaps all these things and more, served him so well that his renown was as renowned as his songs and poems. Fame feeds itself, a serendipity glutton of the moment prescient in publicity.

For such a figure, no exaggeration can be overstated, and the glean of modesty rests in uneasily thin veneer upon a consummated self-adoration that abides the presumption of profundity with all the veracity of that which is truly profound. And to this comment my personal failure as a poet has no bearing whatsoever. Why, I have never viewed words as worthy weapons, having so many others of far more permanent efficacy at my disposal.

Indeed, as I look upon myself at this fire upon the twenty-third night, I see a young(ish) poet of modest regard, scant of pate and so casting nothing of the angelic silhouette upon yonder tent wall as Nifty Gum's cascading curls of thick auburn hair achieve without his giving it a moment's thought, as the gifted rarely if ever regard their gifts except in admiration, or, more deliciously, of admiration in witnessing the admiration of others for all that which is of himself, be it voice or word or hair.

No, I am retracted unto myself, as was my wont in those times, the adventurer none knew, a teller of tales to defy the seam of joinings between those I spun in the Great Dry all those years ago, and this tale that I spin now.

Lives hang in the balance at every moment, in every instant, for life itself is a balance, but sometimes the sky is bright overhead and brilliant with sun and heat and sometimes the sky is darkness with the cold spark of stars dimmed by mistral winds. We see this as the wheel of the heavens, when such a belief is only our failed imagination, for it is us who wheel, like a beetle clinging to a spinning ring, and we are what mark the passing of days.

I see myself then, younger than I am, younger than I have ever been. This is my tale and it is his tale both. How can this be?

But then, what is a soul but the mapping of each and every wheel?

Upon such stately musings rests lightly, one hopes, this addendum. On the twenty-third day just past, the grim mottle of travelers came upon a stranger walking alone. Starved and parched, Apto Canavalian was perhaps in his last moments, and as such might well have met a sudden and final demise at the hands of the Nehemothanai and pilgrims, but for one salient detail. Through cracked lips that perhaps only filled out with a steady diet of wine and raw fish, Apto made it known that he was not a pilgrim of any sort. No, more an adjudicator in spirit if not profession (aspirations notwithstanding), Apto Canavalian was among the elite of elites in the spectrum of intellectualia, a shaper of paradigms, a prognosticator of popularity in the privileged spheres of passing judgement. He was, in short, one of the select judges for The Century's Greatest Artist.

His mule had died of some dreaded pox. His servant had strangled himself in tragic mishap one night of private pleasuring *and now lay buried in a bog well north of the Great Dry. Apto had made this journey at his own expense, the invitation from Farrog's mystical organizers sadly lacking in remuneration, and had nothing left of his stores save one dusty bottle of vinegarish plonk (and, it soon became known, his dread state of dehydration had more to do with the previous nine bottles than with a dearth of water).*

If artists possessed true courage (and this is doubtful) their teeth-bared defense of Apto's life in the moments following his discovery would do well as admirable proof, but so often in life does one mistake desperation and self-interest for courage, for in mien both are raw and indeed, appalling.

Even venerable Tulgord Vise withdrew before the savage display of barely human snarls. In any case, the vote had already been concluded.

The night is younger than you might think, and the tale now lies before us, an enormous log of mysterious origins quick to drink flames from the bed of coals, and the fat sizzles and the circle is drawn tight save the Dantoc who remains, as ever, within her carriage.

Let us, for convenience, list them once more. Apto Canavalian, newly arrived and perhaps more pallid than salvation would invite. Calap Roud, an artist with a century of mediocrity lifting him to minuscule heights. Avas Didion Flicker, venerable voice of this modest retelling. Purse Snippet, demure in the sultry flare of flames, her eyes haunted as dying candles. Brash Phluster, destined as first to speak in the circle only moments away, sitting like a man on an ant hill, feverish of regard and clammy with sweat. Nifty Gum, redoubtable in his reclination, polished boots gleaming at the ends of his outstretched legs upon which are draped two of his Entourage, Oggle Gush, her lashes brushing in every slow blink the precious bulb of Nifty's flower, and Sellup, brow awiggle like a caterpillar on a burning twig, whilst Pampera shifts to a new pose artful in breastly impression upon the side of Nifty's auburn-flowing head and what gurgling promise does that single imprisoned ear detect?

Tiny and Flea and Midge Chanter command the bulwark upon one side of the circle, a pugnacious wall wildly bristling and smelling like a teen-aged boy's bedding, and close to Tiny's scabbed hand sits Relish Chanter, lips smeared in grease and casting hooded wanton but unwanted glances my way. Steck Marynd paces off to her right, ghostly in the faded glow of the hearth. Growl might his stomach but damned if he will soothe it in this company of beasts. Well Knight Arpo Relent sits in the shiver of firelit gold glaring at the Chanters while Tulgord Vise picks at his (own) teeth with the point of a dagger, poised as ever for a cutting remark.

At the last seat is our host, and lest we forget his name, it is suited to muscled sartorial commentary, thus stunning the memory to recollect Sardic Thew, avian in repose, cockerel in assuredness though perhaps somewhat rattled by this point in the proceedings.

Thus, and so well chewed this introduction not a babe would choke upon it, one tremulously hopes.

· · ·

The tale begins with sudden words in the light of the fire, the heat laden with watering aroma, and in the gloom beyond three horses shift and snort and the two mules eye them with envy (they look taller than they really are, and those brushed manes are an affront!). The Great Dry is a frost-sheathed wasteland beyond the fiery island, a scrabble of boulders and rocks and stunted shrubs. The carriage creaks with inner motion and perhaps one rheumy eye is pressed to a crack in the curtains, or an ear perched upon dainty hopes cocked in the folded crenellations of a peep-hole.

And of the air itself, dread is palpable and diluvean.

A Recounting of the
Twenty-third Night

"But listen! Whose tale is this?" So demanded Brash Phluster, a man who was of the height that made short men despise him on principle. His hair was natty and recalcitrant, but fulsome. He had teeth aligned in a mostly even row, full lips below a closely trimmed moustache and above a closely trimmed beard. It was a mouth inclined to pout, a face commissioned for self-pity, and of his nose nothing will be said.

Declamation ringing in the night air, Brash awaited a challenge but none came. We may list the reasons, as they could be of some significance. Firstly, twenty-three days of desperate deprivation and then horror had wearied us all. Secondly, the pull-ward weight of necessity was proving heavy indeed, at least for the more delicate among us. Thirdly, there was the matter of guilt, a most curious yoke that should probably be examined at length, but then, there is no need. Who, pray tell, is unfamiliar with guilt? In punctuated pointedness, fat snapped upon coals and almost everyone flinched.

"But I need a rest and besides, it's time for the critical feasting."

Ah, the critical feasting. I nodded and smiled though none noticed.

Brash wiped his hands on his thighs, shot Purse a glance and then shifted about to make himself more comfortable, before saying, "Ordig's only claim to artistic genius amounted to a thousand mouldy scrolls and his patron's cock in hand. Call yourself an artist and you can get away with anything. Of course, as everyone knows, shit's fertile soil, but for what? That's the question."

The fire spat sparks. The smoke gusted and swung round, stinging new sets of eyes.

Brash Phluster's face, all lit orange and flush and lively, floated like a thing disembodied in the hearth's light; his charcoal cloak with its silver ringlets shrouded him below the neck, which was probably just as well. That head spouting all its words could just as easily be sitting on a stick, and it was still a wonder that it wasn't.

"And Aurpan, well, imagine the audacity of his *Accusations of a Guilty Man*. What a heap of tripe. Guilty? Oh, aye. Guilty of being utterly talentless. It's important—and I know this better than anyone—it's important to bear in mind the innate denseness of the common people, and their penchant to forgive everything but genius. Aurpan was mercifully immune to such risks, which was why everyone loved him."

Flea Chanter grunted. "Give that leg a turn, someone."

Brash was closest to the spit but naturally he made no move. Sighing loudly, Mister Must Ambertroshin leaned forward and took hold of the cloth-wrapped handle. The crackling, sizzling haunch was weighty, inexpertly skewered, but he managed it after a few tries. He sat back, glanced round guiltily, but no one met his eyes.

Darkness, the flames' uncertain light and the smoke were all gifts of mercy this night, but still the stomach lowered heavy and truculent. No one was hungry. This cooked meat would serve the morrow, the aching journey through a strangely emptied Great Dry, the twenty-fourth day in which we travelers felt abandoned by the world, the last left alive, and there was the fear that the Indifferent God was no longer indifferent. Were we the forgotten, the sole survivors of righteous judgement? It was possible, but not, I fair decided as I eyed the leg over the flames, likely.

"So much for Ordig and Aurpan," said Tulgord Vise. "The question is, who do we eat tomorrow night?"

Critical feasting being what it is, sated and indeed bloated satisfaction is predicated upon the artist on the table, as it were. More precisely, the artist must be dead. Will be dead. Shall be naught else but dead. Limbs lie still and do not lash back. Mouth resides slack and rarely opens in affronted expostulation (or worse, vicious cut the razor's wit, hapless corpses strewn all about). The body moves at the nudge only to fall still once more. Prods elicit nothing. Pokes evoke no twitch. Following all these tests, the subject is at last deemed safe to excoriate and rend, de-bone and gut, skin and sunder. Sudden discovery of adoration is permitted, respect acceptable and its proud announcement laudable. Recognition is at last accorded, as in "I recognise that this artist is dead and so finally deserving the accolade of 'genius,' knowing too that whatever value the artist achieved in life is now aspiring in worth tenfold and more." Critical feasting being what it is.

Well Knight Arpo Relent was the first to speak on the matter (what matter? Why, this one). There had been desultory discussion of horses and mules, satisfaction not forthcoming. Resources had been pooled and found too shallow. Stomachs were clenching.

"There are too many artists in the world as it is, and that statement is beyond challenge," and to add veracity to the pronouncement's sanctity (since the gaggle of artists had each and all shown signs of sudden alertness), Arpo Relent settled a gauntlet-sheathed hand upon the pommel of one of his swords. The moment in which argument was possible thus passed. "And since we among the Nehemothanai, whose cause is most just and whose need is both dire and pure, so as to speak in the one voice of honourable necessity, since we, then, require our brave and loyal mounts; whilst it is equally plain that the Dantoc's carriage can proceed nowhere without the mules, we are at the last faced with the hard truth of survival."

"You mean we need to eat somebody." So said I at this juncture, not because I was especially dense, but speaking in the interest of pith (as one has no doubt already observed in the tale thus far). "Say it plain" has always been my motto.

To my crass brevity Arpo Relent frowned as if in disappointment. What artist asks such a thing? What artist lacks the intellectual subtlety to stroke the kitty of euphemism? When the game shall not be played, fun shall not be had. The nature of 'fun' in this particular example? Why, the "fun" of sly self-justification for murder, of course, and what could be more fun than that?

Tiny Chanter was the first to play, with a tiny grin and a piggy regard for the poor artists who now stood miserable as sheep in a pen watching the axeman cometh. "But which one first, Relent? Fat to skinny? Obnoxious to useless? Ugly to pretty? We need a system of selection is what we need. Flea?"

"Aye," Flea agreed.

"Midge?"

"Aye," Midge agreed.

"Relish?"

"I like the one with the shaved head."

"To eat first?"

"What?"

Tiny glared at me. "I warned you earlier, Flicker."

At some juncture in discourse with a thug, one comes to

the point where any uttered word shall obtain as sole justification for violence. It is not the word itself that matters. It is not even the speaking thereof. Indeed, nothing of the world outside the thick skull and murky matter it contains is at all relevant. There is no cause and no effect. No, what has occurred is the clicking of a gear wheel, a winding down to the moment of release. The duration is fixed. The process is irreversible.

Resigned, I waited for Tiny Chanter's pique to detonate.

Instead, Relish said, "They should tell stories."

Steck Marynd took this moment to snort, and it was an exquisite snort in that it clearly counted as the first vote on the matter.

Tiny blinked, and blinked again. One could see the tumult of confusion whisk clouds over his brutal visage, and then his grin broadened, frightening away all the clouds. "Flea?"

"Aye."

"Midge?"

"Aye."

"Knight Relent, you happy with that?"

"I am 'Sir' to you."

"Was that a 'yes'?"

"I think it was," said Flea. "Midge?"

"Oh aye, that was a 'yes' all right."

At this moment Tulgord Vise, Mortal Sword to the Sisters, stepped into the understandable gap between the Nehemothanai and the limpid artists (of which, at this juncture, I blithely count myself). He blew out his cheeks (his upper ones) and stretched a measured regard upon all those gathered, including the host whose name momentarily escapes me, Mister Must, Purse Snippet and the Entourage (poor Apto was yet to arrive). One presumes this was meant to establish Tulgord's preeminence as the final arbiter in the matter (yes, this matter), but of course he too possessed but a single vote, and so the issue was perhaps, for him, one of moral compass. Clearly, he saw in this moment the necessity of justification, and upon ethical concerns who else but Tulgord Vise to dispense adjudication?

Well, how about the victims?

But the retort is equally quick, to be found in the puerile weaponry all within easy reach of those with nothing to lose and everything to gain. Since when do ethics triumph power? So uneven was this debate no one bothered to troop it out for trampling. Accordingly, Tulgord's posturing was met with all the indifference it deserved, a detail entirely lost on him.

The nightly procession was thus determined, as we artists would have to sing not to be supper. Ironically, alas, the very first victim had no tale to attempt at all, for his crime at this moment was to object, with all the terror of a lifetime being picked last in every children's game he ever played, and some memories, as we all know, stay sharp across a lifetime. "Just eat the damned horses!"

But Arpo Relent shook his head. "There is no question of any more votes," he said. "As any one of proper worth would agree, a knight's horse is of far greater value than any poet, bard or sculptor. It's settled. The horses don't get eaten." And he glowered as was his wont following everything he said.

"But that's just—"

It is safe to say that the word this nameless artist intended was "stupid" or "insane" or some other equally delectable and wholly reasonable descriptive. And as added proof when his severed head rolled almost to my feet following the savage slash of Tulgord Vise's blessed sword, the mouth struggled to form its thoughtful completion. Ah, thus did the memory stay sharp.

The first poet, having been killed so succinctly, was butchered and eaten on the eleventh night upon the Great Dry. The sixteenth night saw another follow, as did the twentieth night. Upon the twenty-second night the vote was taken following Arpo's raising of the notion of mid-day meals to keep up one's strength and morale, and so a second artist was sacrificed that night. At that time the ritual of critical feasting began, instigated by a shaky Brash Phluster.

Two more hapless poets, both bards of middling talents, gave the performance of their lives on that night.

At this point, listeners among you, perhaps even you, might raise an objecting hand (not the first one you say? I wasn't paying attention). Thirty-nine days upon the Great Dry? Surely by now, with only a few days away from the ferry landing below the plateau, the need for eating people was past? And of course you would be right, but you see, a certain level of comfort had been achieved. In for a pinch in for a pound, as some sated bastard once said. More relevantly, thirty-nine days was the optimum crossing, and we were far from optimum, at least to begin with. Does this suffice? No, of course it doesn't, but whose tale is this?

Ordig now resided in bellies with a weighty profundity he never achieved in life, while Aurpan's last narrative was technically disconnected and stylistically disjointed, being both raw and overdone. The critical feasting was complete and the artists numbered four, Purse Snippet being given unanimous dispensation, and by the host's judgement sixteen nights remained upon the Great Dry.

While talent with numbers could rarely be counted among the artist's gifts, it was nonetheless clear to all of us sad singers that our time upon this world was fast drawing to a close. Yet with the arrival of dusk this made no less desperate our contests.

Brash Phluster licked his lips and eyed Apto Canavalian for a long moment, before drawing a deep breath.

"I was saving this original dramatic oratory for the last night in Farrog, but then, could I have a more challenging audience than this one here?" And he laughed, rather badly.

Apto rubbed at his face as if needing to convince himself that this was not a fevered nightmare (as might haunt all professional critics), and I do imagine that, given the option, he would have fled into the wastes at the first opportunity, not that such an opportunity was forthcoming given Steck Marynd and his perpetually cocked crossbow which even now rested lightly on his lap (he'd done with his pacing by this time).

In turn, Brash withdrew his own weapon, a three-string lyre, which he set to tuning, head bent over the instrument and face twisted in concentration. He plucked experimentally, then with flourish, and then experimentally again. Sweat glistened in the furrows of his brow, each bead reflecting the hearth's flames. When those seated began growing restless he nudged one wooden peg one last time, and then settled back.

"This is drawn from the Eschologos sequence of Nemil's Redbloom Poets of the Third Century." He licked his lips again. "Not to say I stole anything. Inspired, is what I mean, by those famous poets."

"Who were they again?" Apto asked.

"Famous," Brash retorted, "that's who they were."

"I mean, what were their names?"

"What difference would that make? They sang famous poems!"

"Which ones?"

"It doesn't matter! They were the Redbloom Poets of Nemil! They were famous! They were from the time when bards and poets were actually valued by everyone! Not pushed aside and forgotten!"

"But you've forgotten their names, haven't you?" Apto asked.

"If you never heard of them how would you know if I knew their names or not? I could make up any old names and you'd just nod, being a scholar and all! I'm right, aren't I?"

Calap Roud was shaking his head but there was a delighted glimmer in his eyes. "Young Brash, it serves you ill to berate one of the Mantle's judges, don't you think?"

Brash rounded on him. "You don't know their names either!"

"That's true, I don't, but then, I'm not pretending to be inspired by them, am I?"

"Well, you're about to hear inspiration of the finest kind!"

"What was inspiring you again?" Tiny Chanter asked.

Flea and Midge snorted.

Our host was waving his hands about, and it was finally understood that this manic gesturing was intended to capture our collective attentions. "Gentlemen, please now! The Poet wishes to begin, and each must have his or her turn—"

"What 'her'?" demanded Brash. "All the women here got dispensations! Why is that? Is it, perhaps, because everyone eligible to vote happened to be men? Imagine how succulent—"

"Enough of that!" barked Tulgord Vise. "That's disgusting!"

Arpo Relent added, "What it is, is proof of the immoral decrepitude of artists. Everyone knows it's the women who do the eating."

Moments later, in the ensuing silence, the Well Knight frowned. "What?"

"Best begin, Poet," said Steck Marynd in a hunter's growl (and don't they all?).

A wayward ember spun towards Nifty Gum and all three of his Entourage fought to fling themselves heroically into its path, but it went out before it could reach any of them. They settled back, glowering at each other.

Brash strummed the three strings, and began singing in a flat falsetto.

> "In ages long past
> A long time ago
> Before any of us were alive
> Before kingdoms rose from the dust
> There was a king—"

"Hang on," said Tiny. "If it was before kingdoms, how could there be a king?"

"You can't interrupt like that! I'm singing!"

"Why do you think I interrupted?"

"Please," said the host whose name escapes me again, "let the Poet, er, sing."

> *"There was a king*
> *Who name was . . . Gling*
> *Gling of the Nine Rings*
> *That he wore—"*

"On his bling!" Flea sang.

> *"That he wore one each day*
> *Of the week—"*

Apto broke into a coughing fit.

> *"Gling of the Seven Rings*
> *Was a king whose wife*
> *Had died and sad was his sorrow*
> *For his wife was beloved,*
> *A Queen in her own right.*
> *Her tresses were locks*
> *Flowing down long past*
> *Her shapely shoulders and*
> *Long-haired she was and*

Longhair was her name
She who died of grief
Upon the death of their
Daughter and so terrible her grief
She shaved her head and was
Long-haired no longer
And so furious her beloved
Gling that he gathered up
The strands and wove a rope
With which he strangled
Her—oh sorrow!"

The "oh sorrow" declamation was intended to be echoed by the enraptured audience, and would mark the closure of each stanza. Alas, no one was in a ready state to participate, and isn't it curious how laughter and weeping could be so easily confused?

Savagely, Brash Phluster plucked a string and pressed on.

"But was the daughter truly dead?
What terrible secret did King Gling
Her father possess
There in his tower
At the very heart
Of the world's greatest kingdom?
But no, he was a king
Without any terrible secrets,
For his daughter had been

Stolen, and lovely she was,
The princess whose name was
. . . Missingla
And this is her tale known to all
As Missingla's Tale
Beloved daughter of King Gling and
Queen Longhair,
A princess in her own right
Was Missingla of the shapely shoulders
Royal her eye lashes
A jeweled crown her sweet lips"

Oh dear, I just added those two lines. I could not help it, and so I do urge their disregard.

"Was Missingla of the shapely shoulders
Stolen by the king in the kingdom
Beyond the mountains between the lake
In the Desert of Death
Where almost nothing lived
Or could hope to live
Even should we live in hope"

Ah, and again.

"and this king his name was . . . Lope
Who bore a sword twice as tall as he
And the armour of an ogre made of stone
And cruel was his face, evil his eyes,

As he swam the lake at night
To scale the tower to steal her away
Missingla—oh sorrow!"

The Entourage cried, *"Oh sorrow!"* and even Purse Snippet smiled over her secretive cup of tea.

"But she was waiting oh yes, for
Cruel and evil as he was, so too rich
Beyond all measure ruling the world's
Richest kingdom beyond the mountains
And so not stolen at all, sweet daughter
No! Missingla Lope they swam away!"

In the chaos that ensued, Brash thrashed at the strings of the lyre until one broke, the taut gut snapping up to catch him in the left eye. Steck's crossbow, cursed with a nervous trigger, accidentally released, driving the quarrel through the hunter's right foot, pinning it to the ground. Purse sprayed a startlingly flammable mouthful of tea into the fire, and in the flare-up Apto flung himself backward with singed eyebrows, rolling off the stone he'd been perched on and slamming his head into a cactus. The host's hands waved frantically since he could no longer breathe. The Entourage was in a groping tangle and somewhere beneath it was Nifty Gum. Tulgord Vise and Arpo Relent were scowling and frowning respectively. Of Tiny Chanter, only the soles of his boots were visible. Midge suddenly stood and said to Flea, "I pissed myself."

By this extraordinary performance Brash Phluster survived

the twenty-third night and so would live through the twenty-fourth night and the following day. And as he opened his mouth to announce that he wasn't yet finished, why, I did clamp my hand over the offending utterance, stifling it in the rabbit hole. Mercy knows a thousand guises, say you not?

Madness, you say? That I should so boldly aver Brash Phluster's suicidal desire to further skin himself? But while confidence is a strange creature, it is no stranger to me. I know well its pluck and princeps. It bears no stretch of perception to note my certain flair in the proceeding of this tale, for here I am, ancient of ways, and yet still alive. Ah, but perhaps I deceive you all with this retroactive posture of assuredness. A fair point, were it not for the fact of its error in every regard. To explain, I possessed even then the quiet man's stake, a banner embedded deep in solid rock, the pennants ever calm no matter how savage the raging storms of worldly straits. It is this impervious nature that has served me so well. That and my natural brevity with respect to modesty.

Upon recovery, whilst in relief Brash Phluster stumbled off to vomit behind some boulders, Calap Roud made to begin his tale. His hands trembled like fish in a tree. His throat visibly tightened, forcing squeaking noises from his gaping mouth.

His eyes bulged like eggs striving to flee a female sea-turtle's egg hole. The vast injustice of Brash Phluster's dispensation was a bright sizzling rage in his visage, a teller's tome of twitches plucking at each and every feature so fecklessly clutched beneath his forehead. He was not holding up well to this terrible pressure, this twill or die. Unraveled his comportment, and in tumbling, climbing pursuit a lifetime of missed moments, creative collapses, blocks and heights not reached, all heaved up at this moment to drown him in a deluge of despair.

He was the cornered jump-mouse, the walls too high, the floor devoid of cracks, and all he could do was bare his tiny teeth in the pointless hope that the slayer looming so cruelly over him was composed of cotton fluff. Ah, how life defends itself! It is enough, oh yes, to shatter even a staked man's heart. But know we all that this modern world is one without pity, that it revels in the helplessness of others. Children pluck wings and when grown hulking they crush heads and paint rude words on public walls. Decay bays on all sides, still mourning the moon's tragic death. Pity the jump-mouse, for we are ourselves nothing other than jump-mice trapped in the corners of existence.

In his desperation, Calap Roud realized his only hope for survival would be found in the brazen theft of the words of great but obscure artists, and, fortunate for him, Calap possessed a lifetime of envy in the shadow of geniuses doomed to dissolution in some decrepit alley (said demises often carefully orchestrated by Calap himself: a word here, a raised eyebrow there, the faintest shakes of the head and so on. It is of course the task of average talents to utterly destroy their betters, but not until every strip of chewable morsel is stripped from them first). Thus lit by borrowed inspiration, Calap Roud gathered himself and found a sudden glow and calm repose in which to draw an assured breath.

"Gather ye close, then," he began, in the formal fashion of fifty or so years ago, "to this tale of human folly, as all tales of worth do so recount, to the sorrow of men and women alike. In a great age past, when giants crouched in mountain fast-nesses, fur-bedecked and gripping in hard fists the shafts of war spears; when upon the vast plains below glaciers lay like dead things, draining their lifeblood into ever-deepening valleys; when the land itself growled like a bear in the spring, stomach clenched in necessity, a woman of the Imass slowly died, alone, banished from her ken. She was curled in the lee of a boulder left behind by the ice. The furs covering her pale skin were worn and patched. She had gathered about herself thick mosses and wreathes of lichen to fight against the bitter wind. And though at this time none was there to cast regard upon her, she was beautiful in the way of Imass women, sibling to the earth and melt-waters, to the burst of blossoms in the short season. Her hair, maiden braided, was the colour of raw gold. Her face was broad and full-featured, and her eyes were green as the moss in which she huddled."

A worthy theft to my mind, for I knew this tale. Indeed, I knew the poet whose version Calap was now recounting. Stenla Tebur of Aren managed to fashion a dozen epic poems and twenty or so hearth-tales (or garden-tales, as the Aren knew them, having long since abandoned such rustic scenes as sitting round a hearth beneath stars unmarred by city smoke and light), before his untimely death, at the age of thirty-three. The altar upon which he breathed his last, I am told, was naught but grimy cobbles behind the Temple of Burn, and the breath whereof I speak was a wheezing one, thick with consumption. Alcohol and d'bayang had taken this young man's life, for such are the lures of insensate escape to the tormented artist that rare is the one who deftly avoids such fatal traps. T'was not fame that killed him, alas (for, I would boldly state, death in the time of fame is not as tragic as it might seem, for lost potential is immortal; far greater the sorrow and depression upon hearing of a once-famous life ending in the obscurity of the obsolete). Stenla had given up his siege upon the high and solid walls of legitimacy, manned as it was by legions of jaded mediocrities and coddled luminaries. Forays of vicious rejection had crushed his spirit, until senseless oblivion was all he sought, and found.

"What terrible crime had so cruelly cast her out from her own people?" Calap went on, quoting word for word and thus impressing me with his memory. "The wind howled with the voices of a thousand spirits, each and all bemoaning this fair maiden's fate. Tears from the sky lost the warmth of life and so drifted down as flakes of snow. The great herds in the distance had wandered down to the valley flanks to escape the wind and its dread voices of sorrow. She curled alone, dying."

"But why?" demanded Sellup, earning venomous glares from Pampera and Oggle Gush, for in showing interest in a tale not told by Nifty Gum she was committing a gross betrayal, and even the Great Artist himself was frowning at Sellup. "Why did they leave her like that? That was evil! And she was good, wasn't she? A good person! Pure of heart, an innocent—she had to be! Oh, this is a terrible fate!"

Calap raised a hand in which was cupped borrowed wisdom. "Soon, my dear, all will be known."

"Don't wait too long! I don't like long stories. Where's the action? You've already gone on too long!"

And to that criticism Pampera, Oggle and Nifty all nodded. What is it to trust so little in the worth of a tale well and carefully told? What doth haste win but breathless stupidity? Details of import? *Bah!* Cry these flit-flies. Measures of pace and the thickening of the mat into which the awl must weave? Who cares? Chew into rags and be on to the next, spitting as you go! I look upon the young and see a generation of such courage as to dare nothing more than the ankle-deep, and see them standing proud and arrogant upon the thin shorelines of unknown seas—and to call this living! Oh, I know, it is but an old man's malaise, but to this very moment I still see Sellup and her wide-eyed idiocy, I still hear her impatience and the smack of her lips and the gulp of her breaths, a young woman who could pant herself unconscious in her haste to see her mind transported . . . elsewhere. A stutter of steps, a stagger of impetus, oh, so much she missed!

"Would she lie there unto death," Calap asked, "nameless and unknown? Is this not the darkest tragedy of all? To die in anonymity? To pass from the world unremarked, beneath the notice of an entire world? Oh, the flies wait to lay their eggs. The capemoths flutter like leaves in nearby branches, and in the sky the tiny spots that are ice vultures slowly grow larger with their cargo of endings. But these are the mindless purveyors of mortality and nothing more than that. Their voice is the whisper of wings, the clack of beaks and the snip of insect mouths. It is fey epitaph indeed."

Steck Marynd limped close to the fire and set down another branch collected from somewhere. Flames licked the hoary bark and found it to their liking.

"So we must turn back, outracing the cool sun of spring to the colder sun of winter, and we see before us a huddle of huts, humped upon the bones and tusks of tenag, thick bhederin hides stretched tight over the skeletal frames. The camp crouches not upon the highest hills overlooking the valley, nor upon the banks of the melt-water stream in the basin of the valley itself. No, it clings to a south-facing terrace a little more than halfway up the valley side. The wind's fiercest force is cut in this place and the ground is dry underfoot, draining well into the soggy flats flanking the stream. The Imass were greatly skilled at such things; perhaps indeed their wisdom was a bred thing, immune to true learning, or it may instead be true that those not yet severed from the earth know full the precious secrets of harmony, of using only what is given—"

"Get on with it!" shouted Sellup, the words jumbled by the knuckle bones she was sucking clean. Spitting one out she popped another one in. Her eyes shone like candle flames awakened by a drunkard's breath. "It was a stupid camp. That's all. I want to know what's going to happen! Now!"

Calap nodded. Never argue with a member of one's audience.

Well, perhaps he believed that. For myself, and after much

rumination on the matter, I would suggest the following qualifiers. If that member of the audience is obnoxious, uninformed, dim, insulting, a snob, or drunk, then as far as I am concerned, they are fair game and, by their willingness to engage the artist in said contest, should expect none other than surgical savaging by said artist. Don't you think?

"These Imass in this camp had suffered a terrible winter. Their hunters could find little game, and the great flocks of birds were still weeks away. Many of the elders had walked off into the white to save the lives of their children and grand-children, for winter spoke to them in a secret language only the aged understand. "In life's last days, the white and the cold will lie in the bed of the old." So said the wise among them. Yet, even for this sacrifice, the others weakened with each day. The hunters could not range as far as once they could before ex-haustion turned them back. Children had begun eating the hides that kept them warm at night, and now fevers raced among them.

"She was out, upon the high ridge overlooking the camp, collecting the last autumn's mosses where the winds had swept the snows away, and so was the first to see the approaching stranger. He came down from the north, thickly clad in tenag furs. The long bone-grip of a greatsword rose behind his left shoulder. His head was bared to the winds at his back, and she could see that he was dark, stone-skinned and black-haired. He dragged a sled in his wake.

"In the time before he drew closer, hard thoughts rattled in her mind. They could turn no stranger away in times of need. This was a law among her kind. Yet this warrior was a big man, taller than any Imass. His hunger would be a deep pit, and weakened as her clan's warriors now were, the stranger could take all he wanted if he so chose. And more, she was troubled by that sled, for bundled as it was, she knew it bore a body. If it lived it would need caring. If dead, the warrior was delivering a curse upon her people."

"A curse?" Sellup asked. "What kind of curse?"

Calap blinked.

Seeing that he had no specific response to this question, I cleared my throat. "Death *leaves* such camps, Sellup, and that is well and as it should be. This is why the elders, when they decide it is time to die, walk out into the white. It is also why all kills are butchered well away from the camp itself, so that only meat, hide and bones intended to be made into tools—gifts to life one and all—enter the camp. Should death come *into* the camp, the hosts are cursed and must immediately make propitiations to the Reaver and his demon slaves, lest Death find the camp to his liking and so make it his home. When the Reaver finds a home, the living soon die, do you see?"

"No."

Sighing, I said, "It is one of those rules couched in spiritual guise that, in truth, has a more secular purpose. To bring someone dead or dying into a small camp is to invite contagion and disease. Among such a close-knit clan, any infection is likely to claim them all. Thus, the Imass had certain rules to prevent such a thing occurring, yet those rules, alas, conflicted with that of never turning a guest away in times of need. So the woman was with troubled thoughts, yes?"

"But he's evil—he has to be! He's the Reaper himself!"

"Reaver," I corrected, "or so the citizens of Aren so call the Lord of Death."

Calap flinched and would not thereafter meet my eyes. "So she stood, trembling, as the stranger, who had clearly chosen her as his destination, now drew up to halt nine paces distant. She saw at once that he was not Imass. He was from the mountain heights. He was Fenn, a giant of Tartheno Toblakai blood. And too, she saw that he bore the marks of battle. Slash wounds that had cut through the woolly Tenag hide had encrusted the slices with the warrior's own blood. His right hand and forearm were blackened with old gore, and so too was his face spattered in violent maps.

"He was silent for a time, his heavy eyes held upon her, and then he spoke. He said—"

"Finish this tomorrow night," Tiny Chanter said, cracking a wide yawn.

"That's not how it works," Tulgord Vise said in a growl. "We can't very well vote if one of the tales remains incomplete."

"I want to hear more, don't I?" Tiny retorted. "But I'm falling asleep, right? So, we get the rest tomorrow night."

I noticed that Nifty Gum was endeavouring to catch my eye. In response I raised my brows and shrugged.

Oggle Gush said then, "But I want to hear Nifty's story!"

Nifty made to silence the girl, if the twitching of his hands and their spasmodic clutching (miming throttling a throat) was any indication, though who but Nifty could truly say?

"Tomorrow during the day then! Same for the other one—we got time and since there ain't nothing to see anyway and nothing to do but walk, let's have 'em entertain us till sunset! No, it's settled and all, ain't it, Flea?"

"Aye," said Flea. "Midge?"

"Aye," said Midge.

"But the night is still young," objected Arpo Relent, and one could tell from a host of details in his demeanor that the sudden dispatch of impending death-sentences had frustrated some pious repository of proper justice within his soul, and now in his face there was the blunt belligerence of a thwarted child.

Purse Snippet then surprised us all by saying, "I will tell a tale, then."

"My lady," gasped the host, "it was settled—there is no need—"

"I would tell a tale, Sardic Thew, and so I shall." With this assertion muting us all she then hesitated, as if startled by her own boldness. "Words are not my talent, I admit, so forgive me if I stumble on occasion."

Who could not but be forgiving?

"This too belongs to a woman," she began, her eyes on the flames, her elegantly-fingered hands encircling her clay vessel. "Loved and worshiped by so many—" she sharply looked up. "No, she was no dancer, nor a poet, nor actress nor singer. Hers was a talent born to, yet not one that could be further honed. In truth, it was not a talent at all, but rather the gathering of chance—lines and curves, symmetries. She was, in short, beautiful, and from that beauty her life was shaped, her future preordained. She would marry well, above her station, and in that marriage she would be the subject of adoration, as if she was a precious object of art, until such time that age stole her beauty, whereupon her fine home would become a tomb of sorts, her bedroom rarely frequented at night by her husband, whose vision of beauty remained forever youthful.

"There would be wealth. Fine foods. Silks and fetes. There would be children, perhaps, and there would be something . . . something wistful, there in her eyes at the very end."

"That's not a story!" Oggle Gush said.

"I have but begun, child—"

"Sounds more like an end to me, and don't call me child, I'm not a child," and she looked to Nifty for confirmation, but he was instead frowning at Purse Snippet, as if seeking to understand something.

Purse Snippet resumed her tale, but her eyes were now bleak as she gazed into the fire. "There are quests, in a person's life, that require no steps to be taken. No journey across strange landscapes. There are quests where the only monsters are the shadows in a bedroom, the reflection in a mirror. And one has no companions hale and brave to stand firm at one's side. This is a thing taken in solitude. She was loved by many, yes. She was desired by all who saw the beauty of her, but of beauty within herself, she could see nothing. Of love for the woman she was inside, there was none. Can the pulp of the fruit admire the beauty of its skin? Can it even know that beauty?"

"Fruits don't have eyes," said Oggle Gush, rolling her own. "This is stupid. You can't have quests without mountain passes and dangerous rivers to cross, and ogres and demons and wolves and bats. And there's supposed to be friends of the hero who go along and fight and stuff, and get into trouble so the hero has to save them. Everyone knows that."

"Oggle Gush," Apto Canavalian said (now that he'd done plucking cactus spikes from the back of his head), "kindly shut that useless hole in your face. Purse Snippet, please, go on."

Whilst Oggle gaped and mawped and blinked like an owl in a vice, Steck Marynd appeared to add more wood to the fire and it occurred to me that the stolid, grim ranger was indeed doing woodly things, which meant that all was well, though of greater tasks and higher import something must obtain with this personage, sooner or later. One hopes.

"She would stand upon a balcony overlooking the canal where the gramthal boats plied carrying people and wares. Butterflies in the warm air would lift as if on sounds to gather round her." She faltered then, for some unknown reason, and drew a few breaths before continuing, "and though all who chanced to look up, all who set eyes upon her, saw a maiden of promise, indeed, a work of art posed thus upon that balcony, why, in her soul there was war. There was anguish and suffering, there was dying to an invisible enemy, one that could cut the feet beneath every mustered argument, every armoured affirmation. And the dark air was filled with screams and weeping, and upon no horizon did dawn make promise, for this was a night unending and a war without respite.

"A lifetime, she would tell you, is a long time to bleed. There is paint for pallor, the hue of health to hide the ashen cheeks, but the eyes cannot be disguised. There you will find, if you look closely, the tunnels to the battlefield, to that unlighted place where no beauty or love can be found."

The fire ate wood, coughed smoke. No one spoke. The mirror was smudged, yes, but a mirror nonetheless.

"Had she said but a single word," muttered someone (was it me?), "a thousand heroes would have rushed to her aid. A thousand paths of love to lead her out of that place."

"That which cannot love itself cannot give love in return," she replied. "So it was with this woman. But, she knew in her heart, the war must end. What devours within will, before long, claw its way to the surface, and the gift of beauty will falter. Dissolution rots outward. The desperation grew within her. What could she do? Where in her mind could she go? There was, of course," and inadvertently her eyes dropped to the cup in her hands, "sweet oblivion, and all the masks of escape as offered by wine, smoke and such, but these are no more than the paths of decay—gentle paths, to be sure, once one gets used to the stench. And before long, the body begins to fail. Weakness, illness, aching head, a certain lassitude. Death beckons, and by this alone one knows that one's soul has died."

"My lady," Tulgord Vise ventured, "this tale of yours demands a knight, sworn to goodness. Tis a fair damsel in deepest distress—"

"Two knights!" cried Arpo Relent, although with a zeal that sounded, well, forced.

Tulgord grunted. "There is only one *one* knight in this tale. The other knight is the other knight."

"There can be two knights! Who is to say there can't?"

"Me. I'm to say. I will allow two knights, however. The real one, me. The other one, you."

Arpo Relent's face was bright red, as if swallowing flames. "I'm not the other knight! You are!"

"When I cut you in two," Tulgord said, "you can be two knights all by yourself."

"When you cut me in two you won't know which way to turn!"

Silence has flavour, and this one was confused, as follow certain statements that, in essence, make no sense whatsoever, yet nonetheless possess a peculiar logic. Such was this momentary interlude composed of frowns, clouds and blinks.

Purse Snippet spoke. "She came to a belief that the gods set alight a spark in every soul, the very core of a mortal spirit, which mayhap burns eternal, or, in less forgiving eyes, but gutters out once the flesh has fallen beyond the last taken breath. To sharpen her need, she chose the latter notion. Now, then, there was haste and more: there was a true edge of possible redemption. If in our lives, we are all that we have and ever will have, then all worth lies in the mortal deed, in that single life."

"A woman without children, then," Apto murmured.

"What gift passing such beauty on? No, she was yet to marry, yet to take any seed. Only within her mind had she so aged, seeing an end both close and far off, ten years in a century, ten centuries in an instant. Resolved, then, she would seek to journey to find that spark. Could it be scoured clean, enlivened to such bright fire that all flaws simply burned away? She would see, if she could.

"But what manner this journey? What landscape worth the telling?" And upon that moment her eyes, depthless tunnels, found me. "Will you, kind sir, assemble the scene for my poor tale?"

"Honoured," said I mostly humbly. "Let us imagine a vast plain, broken and littered. Starved of water and bare of animals. She travels alone and yet in company, a stranger among strangers. All she is she hides behind veils, curtains of privacy, and awaiting her as awaiting the others, there is a river, a flowing thing of life and benison. Upon its tranquil shores waits redemption. Yet it remains distant, with much privation in between. But what of those who travel with her? Why, there are knights avowed to rid the world of the unseemly. In this case, the unseemly personages of two foul sorcerors of the darkest arts. So too there are pilgrims, seeking blessing from an idle god, and a carriage travels with them and hidden within it there is a face, perhaps even two, whom none have yet to see—"

"Hold!" growled Steck Marynd, looming out of the gloom, crossbow held at rest but cocked across one forearm. "See how the colour has left the face of this woman? You draw too close, sir, and I like it not."

Mister Ambertroshin relit his pipe.

"Lacks imagination," purred Nifty Gum. "Allow me, Lady Snippet. The village of her birth is a small holding upon the rocky shores of a fjord. Beyond the pastures of her father the king, crowded forests rear up mountain sides, and in a deep fastness there sleeps a dragon, but most restlessly, for she had given birth to an egg, one of vast size, yet so hard was the shell that the child within managed to no more than break holes for its legs and arms, and with its snout it had rubbed thin the shell before its eyes, permitting it a misty regard of the world beyond. And, alas, the egg monster had escaped the cavern and now roved down between the black trees, frightened and lost and so most dangerous.

"In its terrible hunger it has struck now in the longhouse of the king, rolling flat countless warriors as they slept ensorcelled by the child's magic. Woe, bewails the king! Who can save them? Then came the night—"

"What knight?" Tulgord demanded.

"No, night, as in the sun's drowning in darkness—"

"The knight drowned the sun?"

"No, fair moon's golden rise—"

"He's mooning the sun?"

"Excuse me, what?"

"What's the knight doing, damn you? Cracking that egg in half, I wager!"

"The sun went down—that kind of night!"

"Why didn't you say so?" Tulgord Vise snorted.

"And the monster set a deep magic upon the longhouse. Bursting down the stout door—"

"He ran into the knight!"

"No, instead, he fell in love with the princess, for as she was ugly on the inside, he was ugly on the outside—"

"I'd suspect," Apto said, "he'd be pretty ugly on the inside, too. Dragon spawn, trapped in there. No hole for the tail? He'd be neck deep in shit and piss. Why—"

Brash Phluster, working on his second supper, having lost the first one, pointed a finger bone at Nifty and, with a greasy smirk, said, "The Judge is right. You need to explain things like that. The details got to make sense, you know."

"Magic answers," snapped Nifty with a toss of his locks. "The monster walked into the main hall and saw her, the princess, and he fell in love. But knowing how she would view him with horror, he was forced to keep her in an enchanted sleep, through music piped out from the various holes in his shell—"

"He farted her a magic song?" Apto asked.

"He piped her a magic song, which made her rise as would one sleep-walking, and so she followed him out from the hall."

"What's that story got to do with Purse Snippet's?" Was that my question? It was.

"I'm getting to that."

"You're getting to the point where I vote we spit you on the morrow," said Tulgord Vise.

Arpo Relent agreed. "What a stupid story, Nifty. An egg monster?"

"There is mythical precedent for—"

"Make your silence deep, poet," warned Steck Marynd. "My Lady Snippet, do you wish any of these pathetic excuses for poets to resume their take on your tale?"

Purse Snippet frowned, and then nodded. "Flicker's will suit me, I think. A river, the promise of salvation. Strangers all, and the hidden threat of the hunted—tell me, poet, are they closer to their quarry than any might imagine?"

"Many are the stratagems of the hunted, My Lady, to confound their pursuers. So, who can say?"

"Tell us more of this quest, then."

"A moment, please," said Steck Marynd, his voice grating as if climbing a stone wall with naught but fingernails and teeth. "I see that unease has taken hold of Mister Ambertroshin. He gnaws upon the stem and the glow waxes savage again and again." He shifted the crossbow, his weight fully on the one leg whose foot had not suffered the indignity of a quarrel through it only a short time earlier. "You, sir, what so afflicts you?"

Mister Ambertroshin was long in replying. He withdrew his pipe and examined the chipped clay stem, and then the bowl, whereupon he drew out his leather pouch and pinched out a small amount of stringy rustleaf, which he deftly rolled between two fingers and a thumb before tamping it down into the pipe's blackened bowl. He drew fiercely a half-dozen times, wreathing his lined face in swirling clouds. And then said, "I think I'm going to be sick."

"Ordig was something sour, wasn't he?" Brash Phluster opined, and then he laughed in the manner of a hyena down a hole, even as he wiped grease from his hands.

Grunting, Steck Marynd limped away, and over one shoulder said, "It's suspicious, that's all. Suspicious strange, I mean. Diabolical minds and appalling arrogance, aye, that spells them sure. I need to think on this." And with that off into the darkness he went.

Tulgord Vise was frowning. "Addled wits. That's what comes of living in the woods with the moles and pine beetles. Now then, Flicker, you have a burden to bear with your tale, for it must carry this Lady's charge. Tell us more of the knights."

"They number five in all," did I respond, "though one was counted senior by virtue of skill and experience. Sworn were they to the execution of criminals, and criminality in this case was found in the committal of uncivil behaviour. More specifically, in behaviour that threatened the very foundations of civilization—"

"Just so!" said Arpo Relent, fist striking palm, an unfortunate gesture in that he was wearing gauntlets with studded knuckles but only kid leather upon the palms. His eyes widened in pain.

"Tender pleasures this night for you," commented Apto Canavalian.

Of course Arpo would not permit a single utterance of agony to escape him. So he sat, cringing, jaw muscles bulging, water starting in his eyes.

"As it is known to all," I resumed, "civilization lies at the very heart of all good things. Wealth for the chosen, privilege for the wealthy, countless choices for the privileged. The promise of food and shelter for all the rest, provided they work hard for it. And so on. To threaten to destroy it is, accordingly, the gravest betrayal of all. For, without civilization there is barbarism, and what is barbarism? Absurd delusions of equality, generous distribution of wealth, and settlements where none can hide in anonymity their most sordid selves. It is, in short, a state sure to be deemed chaotic and terrible by the sentinels of civilization, said sentinels being, by virtue of their position, guardians of property more often than not their own. To display utter disdain for civilization, as surely must be the regard of the two mad sorcerers, can only be seen as an affront and a most insistent source of indignation.

"Thus fired with zeal we see our brave knights, sworn one and all to destroy those who would threaten the society that has granted them title and privilege, and what could be more selfless than that?"

Purse Snippet, I saw in aside, was smiling, even as both Tulgord and Arpo made solemn their nods, Arpo having recovered to

some extent from his foray into the melodramatic. Apto Canavalian was smirking. Brash Phluster was dozing, as were Nifty
Gum's entourage of three, whilst their erstwhile paragon was
hair-twirling (one of those habitual gestures that brings to mind
the measured unraveling of intelligence or at least the appearance thereof) and, at the same time, seeking to catch the eye of
Relish Chanter, the last Chanter still awake this night. There
are, it must be said, men of the world who, for all their virility,
will at times confuse the gender of their flirtations. For it is in
my mind the woman who twirls (for how wonderfully attractive
is vacuousness, assuming natural affinities to knee-high morals
and such), and bats lashes with coy obviousness, not the man.
Nifty Gum, alas, having no doubt witnessed endless displays of
said behaviour directed at him, now seemed to believe it was
courting's own language; alas, in giving back what he so com-
monly received, he did little more than awaken Relish's sneer,
Relish being a goodly woman and not inclined to mothering.

"I could speak now of the pilgrims," said I, "but for the ease
of narrative, let it be simply said that all who seek to catch the
eyes of a god, are as empty vessels believing themselves incomplete unless filled, and that said fulfillment is, for some reason,
deemed to be the gift given by some blessed hand not their
own."

"Is there no more to it, then?" so asked Mister Ambertroshin,
who seemed to have recovered his momentary disquiet.

My gesture was one of submission. "Who am I to say, in truth?
Even I can see the lure of utter faith, the zest of happy servitude
to an unknown but infinitely presumptuous cause."

"Presumptuous?"

"Anyone can fill silence with voices, kind driver," I said in reply. "We are most eager inventors, are we not?"

"Ah, I understand. You suggest that religious conviction consists of elaborate self-delusion, that those who hear the words of their god telling them to do this and that, are in fact inventing their certainty as they go."

"I would hazard it all begins," ventured I, "with someone else, a priest or priestess, or the written words of the same, telling them first. The mission needs direction, yes? One serves a purpose, and in the god's silence, who is it that presumes to describe that purpose? If all are lost, the first to shout that he or she has found something will be as a lodestone to others, and their desperation will become the joy of relief. But who is to say that the one who shouted first was not lying? Or mad? Or possessing ambitions of far more secular nature—to wit, how much can I bilk all these fools for?"

Mister Ambertroshin puffed on his pipe. "You do indeed walk a wasteland, sir."

"And does yours look so different?"

"We may agree on the rocks and stones, sir," he replied, "but not their purpose."

"Rocks?" Tulgord said, eyes a little wild. "Stones and purpose? Aye, give me a rock, something for you to trip over, driver, but for me, something to bash in your head."

Mister Ambertroshin blinked. "Why, Mortal Sword, why ever would you do that?"

"Because you're confusing things, that's why! Flicker's telling a story, right? By all meets he must now give voice to the evil whispers seeking ill of our heroes."

"I think he just did," the pipe-puffing old man said.

"The knights hold to honour and purpose and the two are one and the same," proclaimed Tulgord Vise. "While the pilgrims seek salvation. Now, who else travels with the worthy ones? Someone diabolical, no doubt. Speak on, poet, for your life!"

"I hesitate, good knight."

"What?"

"Without the Chanters, there can be no proper vote, can there? And by their collective snores one can presume only that they are insensate to the moment. Lady Snippet, does your need devour all patience?"

She regarded me with some slyness. "Do you promise redemption, poet?"

"I do."

Sudden doubt in her eyes, perhaps even a trembling vulnerability. "Do you?" she asked again, this time in a whisper.

I gave gentle nod.

"It would seem most honourable," suggested Apto, studying me grave and seriously, "that your fate, Flicker, now be made to depend solely upon Purse Snippet's judgement. Should you achieve redemption of the woman in her tale, your life is secured. Should you fail, it is forfeit. This being said, and by all the nods I see it is a notion well-met, it would not do to string her along and so assure your survival. So I pose the following provision. Should she decide, at any time in your telling, that you are simply . . . shall we say, *padding* your narrative, why, one or both of the knights shall swing their swords."

"Wait!" cried Calap Roud. "I am not nodding and this is not well-met—not by me anyway. Can we not all see that Lady

Snippet is a woman of mercy? And not such a soul as would so cruelly condemn someone? This is Flicker's devious mind at work here! He makes a promise he cannot keep, but only to win his life upon this terrible journey! Perhaps indeed they are in cahoots!"

At that the dancer straightened in perfect haughtiness. "Bitter words from you, poet, dredged from a poor and squalid mind. I have performed before the most fickle tyrants, when it was *my* life that was at stake. Of harsh yet true adjudication, I have learned at the feet of masters. Do you think I would dissemble? Do you think I would not cast a most hardened eye upon this man who so boldly promises redemption? Be it understood to all, that Avas Didion Flicker chooses—if he dares—the deadliest of courses in the days ahead!"

So stark and shocking this bridling that all were humbled, and as all eyes now fixed upon me, I knew the truth of this bargain. Did my courage quiver? Did my bowels loosen more than a stomach full of human meat warranted (and yes, Ordig was indeed most sour)? Shall I take this instant to weave the woeful lie? I shall not. Indeed, I make no comment whatsoever, and before that sharp wealth of regard, I tilted head a fraction toward the venerable dancer and said, "I do accept."

And to that she could only gasp.

Weariness soon landed on bat wings, ears twitching, flitting ghostly among us all, and this night was, by silent consensus, done. As I rose to walk watery into the darkness for a few moments of cold desert air and mocking stars, beyond all heat and light from the dying hearth, I drew close about me my threadbare cloak. It is the still moments in which doubts assail the soul. So I'm told.

The notion was untested as soft arms closed about my waist and two full and generous breasts spread across my back. A breathy voice then murmured in my ear, "You're a clever one, aren't you?"

Perhaps not so clever as I believed, as my right hand dropped and stole back to find the outside of her thigh. What is it with men, anyway? To see is as good as to touch when seeing is all we can manage; but to touch is as good as to explode in milky clouds in the spawning stream. "Oh," murmured I, "sweet Relish. Is this wise?"

"My brothers snore, do you hear them?"

"Alas, I do."

"When they're snoring, you can drop rocks on their heads and still they won't wake. I know. I've done it. Big rocks. And when they wake up with knobs and bruises, I just tell them they all knocked heads together last night, and so they get mad at each other and that's that."

"It would seem that I am not the only clever one here."

"That's right, but then, maybe you ain't so smart after all. She'll see you killed, that bitchy dancer, you know that, don't you?"

"It is indeed quite possible."

"So this could be your last night left alive. Let's make it a fun one."

"Who saw you leave the camp?"

"No one. I made sure everyone was bedded down."

"I see. Well, then . . ."

Shall we titter and wing gazes heavenward now? Shall we draw the veil of modesty upon these decorous delicacies? Is it enough to imagine and paint private scenes in the mind? A knowing smile, the flash of bared flesh, a subtle editing of grunts and pinches and shifts as elbows prod and jab? Dreamy our sighs, delicious our ponderings? What's wrong with you?

She straddled my face. The meaty flesh of her thighs closed like the jaws of a toothless leg monster, oozing with suffocating intentions. My tongue discovered places it had never known before, and partook of flavours I wish never to revisit. After some frenzied mashing of orifices that made the bones of my skull creak ominously, she lifted herself clear with an ear-crackling sucking sound, twisted round and descended once more.

There are places in the human body where no man's face belongs, and this fact found its moment of discovery for hapless Avas Didion Flicker at that precise instant. Well, once her fullest intentions were made evident, that is. The heave with which I freed myself was of sufficient vigour as to throw her over my feet and flat on her face upon the stony ground. Her grunt was most becoming. She endeavoured a vicious kick which I deftly dodged as I rolled up and onto her back, forcing both knees up between her legs. Twisting, she flung a handful of sand and gravel into my eyes. Ignoring this ambiguous gesture I took hold of her meaty thighs and lifted them off the ground, and then impaled her most mightily.

She clawed furrows in the hard ground as if swimming for shore, but the riptide of my lust held her fast. It was, assuredly, do or drown for Relish Chanter. Her gasps gusted clouds of dust round her face. She coughed, she hacked, she moaned in the manner of mothers behind the pantry door, and with her hips she bolted like a cow before the bull, only to lunge backward with small animal cries. I leaned forward and wrapped close my arms, hands finding her breasts. I took hold of full nipples and tried to twist them off, failing but not for want of trying to be sure.

As all know, lovemaking is the most gentle art. Sweet sensations, tender strokes of desire, the sudden nearness of hovering lips, a brush of cheeks, the sharing of wine breaths and so on. Clothes peel off languorous and sultry, shadows tease and warmth invites and then drips, and about all the bedding closes to enfold soft and fresh.

Lacking such amenities of the seductive, let the dogs howl. Beneath savagely cold stars, in beds of wiry stunted bushes, broken branches, rocks and buttons of cacti, this was the scrape and gouge of seed's wild spill, a life's banking in a dubious vessel of potential posterity, when said vessel is all there is on offer. Burgeon proud seed! Steal vigorous root in sweetest flesh! Bay with life's triumph! I held her very nearly upside down as I unleashed my hungry stream, and if she didn't weep white tears it is no small miracle.

The reparations that followed were conducted in sated silence.

She combed through her hair to remove the bark, pebbles and saliva. I rubbed my face with sand and would have cut off my own left arm for a bowl of water. We hunted down our wayward clothing, before each in turn staggering off to find our bedding.

Thus ended the twenty-third night upon Crack'd Pot Trail.

A Recounting of the
Twenty-fourth Day

Like rubbing a glossy coat the wrong way, secret amorous escapades can leave the elect parties stirred awry in the wake, although of course there are always exceptions to the condition, and it would appear that, upon the dawn of the twenty-fourth day, both your venerable chronicler and Relish Chanter could blissfully count themselves thus blessed. Indeed, I never slept better, and from Relish's languid feline stretch upon sitting up from her furs, her mind was as unclouded as ever, sweet as unstirred cream upon the milk.

Far more soured the dispositions of the haggard mottle of artists as the sun elbowed its way up between the distant crags to the east. Wretched their miens, woeful their swollen eyes. Harried their hair, disheveled their comportment as sullen they gathered about the embers whilst Steck Marynd revived the flames with sundry fettles of tinder and whatnot. Strips of meat roasted the night before were chewed during the wait for the single small pot of tea to boil awake.

With bared iron fangs, the day promised torrid heat. Already the sun blazed willful and not a single cloud dared intrude upon the cerulean sands of heaven's arena. We stood or sat with the roar of blood in our ears, the silty tea gritty upon our leathery tongues, our hands twitching as if reaching for the journey's end.

From somewhere close came the keening cry of a harashal, the cruel lizard vulture native to the Great Dry. The creature could smell the burnt bone, the raveled flaps of human skin and scalp, the entrails shallowly buried in a pit just upwind of the camp. And with its voice it mocked our golden vigour until we felt nothing but leaden guilt. The world and indeed life itself lives entirely within the mind. We cast the colours ourselves, and every scene of salvation to one man shows its curly-haired backside to another. And so standing together we each stood alone, and that which we shared was unpleasant to all.

With, perhaps, a few exceptions. Rubbing a lump on his temple, Tiny Chanter walked off to fill a hole, humming as he went. Flea and Midge grinned at each other, which they did with unnerving frequency. Both had sore skulls and only moments earlier had been close to drawing knives, the belligerence halted by a warning grunt from Tiny.

Mister Ambertroshin filled a second cup of tea and walked over to the carriage, where a chamber pot awaited him set on the door's step. A single knock and the wooden shutter on the window opened a crack, just wide enough for him to send the cup through, whereupon it snapped shut, locks setting. He collected the chamber pot and set out to dispose of its contents.

Tulgord Vise watched him walk off and then he grunted. "Looked to be a heavy pot for some old lady. See that, Steck? Arpo?"

The forester squinted with slitty eyes, but perhaps that was just the woodsmoke drifting up to enwreathe his weathered face.

Arpo, on the other hand, was frowning. "Well, she took two helpings last night, so it's no wonder."

"Did she now?" and Tulgord Vise glanced over at the carriage. He scratched at his stubbled jaw.

"Must get horrid hot in there," Apto Canavalian mused, "despite the shade. Not a single vent is left open."

Arpo set off to see to his horse, and after a moment Tulgord did something similar. Steck had already saddled his own half-wild mount and it stood nearby, chewing on whatever grasses it could find. Mister Ambertroshin returned with the scoured pot and stored it in the back box, which he then locked. He then attended to the two mules. So too did the others address to sundry chores or, as privilege or arrogance warranted, did nothing but watch the proceedings. Oggle Gush and Pampera set about combing Nifty's golden locks, while Sellup bundled bedding and then laced onto Nifty's feet the artist's knee-high moccasins.

Thus did the camp break and all preparations were made for the trek ahead.

Calap Roud and Brash Phluster came up to me in the course

of such reading. "Listen, Flicker," said Calap in a low voice, "nobody's even told the Chanters about your deal last night, and I'm still of a mind to argue against it."

"Oh, did the Lady's word not convince you then?"

"Why should it?" he demanded.

"Me neither," said Brash. "Why you anyway? She won't even look at me and I'm way better looking."

"This relates to the tale, surely," said I. "A woman such as Purse Snippet would hardly be of such beggarly need as to consider me in any other respect. Brash Phluster, I began a tale and she wishes to hear its end."

"But it's not a believable one, is it?"

To that I could but shrug. "A tale is what it is. Must you have every detail relayed to you, every motivation recounted so that it is clearly understood? Must you believe that all proceeds at a certain pace only to flower full and fulsome at the expected time? Am I slave to your expectations, sir? Does not a teller of tales serve oneself first and last?"

Calap snorted. "I have always argued thus. Who needs an audience, after all. But this situation, it is different, is it not?"

"Is it?" I regarded them both. "The audience can listen, or they can walk away. They can be pleased. They can be infuriated. They can feel privileged to witness or cursed by the same. If I kneel to one I must kneel to all. And to kneel is to surrender and this no teller of tales must ever do. Calap Roud, count for me the times you have been excoriated for your arrogance. To be an artist is to know privilege from both sides, the privilege of creating your art and the privilege in those who partake of it. But even saying such a thing is arrogance's deafening howl, is it not? Yet the audience possesses a singular currency in this exchange. To partake thereof or to not partake thereof. It extends no further for them, no matter how they might wish otherwise. Now, Calap, you say this situation is different, indeed, unique, yes?"

"When our lives are on the line, yes!"

"I have before me my audience of one, and upon her and her alone my life now rests. But I shall not kneel. Do you understand? She certainly understands—I can see that and am pleased by it. How will she judge? By what standards?"

"By that of redemption," said Calap. "It's what you have offered, after all."

"Redemption comes in a thousand guises, and they are sweetest those that come unexpectedly. For now, she will trust me, but, as you say, Calap, at any time she can choose to abandon that trust. So be it."

"So you happily trust your life to her judgement?"

"Happily? No, I would not use that word, Calap Roud. The point is, I will hold to my story, for it is mine and none other's."

Scowling and no doubt confused, Calap turned about and walked away.

Brash Phluster, however, remained. "I would tell you something, Avas Flicker. In confidence."

"You have it, sir."

"It's this, you see." He licked his lips. "I keep beginning my songs, but I never get to finish them! Everyone just votes me dispensation! Why? And they laugh and nobody's supposed to be laughing at all. No, say nothing just yet. Listen!" His eyes were bright with something like horror. "I decided to hide my talent, you see? Hide it deep, save it for the Festival. But then, this happened, and suddenly I realized that I needed to use it, use it to its fullest! But what happened? I'll tell you what happened, Flicker. Now I know why I was damned good at hiding my talent." He clawed at his straggly beard. "It's because I don't have any in the first place! And now I'm sunk! Once they stop laughing, I'm a dead man!"

Such are the nightmares of artists. The gibbering ghosts of dead geniuses (yes, they are all dead). The bald nakedness of some future legacy, chewed down illegible. The torture and flagellation of a soul in crisis. The secret truth is that every artist kneels, every artist sets head down upon the block of fickle opinion and the judgement of the incapable. To be a living artist is to be driven again and again to explain oneself, to justify every creative decision, yet to bite down hard on the bit is the only honourable recourse, to my mind at least. Explain nothing, justify even less. Grin at the gallows, dear friends! The artist that lives and the audience that lives while they live are without relevance! Only those still unborn shall post the script of legacy, whether it be forgotten or canonized! The artist and the audience are trapped together in the now, the instant of mood and taste and gnawing unease and all the blither of fugue that is opinion's facile realm! Make brazen your defiance and make well nested your home in the alley and doorstep or, if the winds fare you well, in yon estate with Entourage in tow and the drool of adoration to soothe your path through the years!

"Dear Brash," said I after this torrid outburst, "worry not. Sing your songs with all the earnestness you possess. What is talent but the tongue that never ceases its wag? Look upon us poets and see how we are as dogs in the sun, licking our own behinds with such tender love. Naught else afflicts us but the vapours of our own worries. Neither sun nor stone heeds human ambition. Kings hire poets to sell them lies of posterity. Be at fullest ease, is it not enough to try? Is desire not sufficient proof? Is conviction not the stoutest shield and helm before wretched judgement? If it is true that you possess the talent of the talentless, celebrate the singularity of your gift! And should you survive this trek, why, I predict your audience will indeed be vast."

"But I won't!"

"You shall. I am sure of it."

Brash Phluster's eyes darted. "But then . . . that means . . . Calap Roud? Nifty Gum?"

Solemn my nod.

"But that won't be enough!"

"It shall suffice. We shall make good time today, better than our host adjudges."

"Do you truly believe so?"

"I do, sir. Now, the others have begun and the carriage is moments from lurching forward. Unless you wish to breathe the dust of its passing, we had best be on, young poet."

"What if Purse hates your story?"

I could but shrug.

Now, it falls upon artists of all ilk to defend the indefensible, and in so doing reveal the utterly defenseless nature of all positions of argument, both yours and mine. Just as every ear bent to this tale is dubious, so too the voice spinning its way down the track of time. Where hides the truth? Why, nowhere and everywhere, of course. Where slinks the purposeful lie? Why, 'tis the lumps beneath truth's charming coat. So, friends, assume the devious and you'll not be wrong and almost half-right, as we shall see.

Not twenty paces along, Tiny Chanter pointed a simian forefinger at Calap Roud and said, "You, finish your story, and if it's no good you're dead."

"Dead," agreed Flea.

"Dead," agreed Midge.

Calap gulped. "So soon?" he asked in a squeak. "Wait! I must compose myself! The Imass woman, dying in the cold, a spin backward in time to the moment when the Fenn warrior, sorely wounded, arrives, sled in tow. Yes, there I left it. There. So." He rubbed at his face, worked his jaw as might a singer or pugilist (wherein for both beatings abound, ah, the fates we thrust upon ourselves!), and then cleared his throat.

"He stood silent before her," Calap began, "and she made gesture of welcome. 'Great Fenn,' said she—"

"What's her name?" Sellup asked.

"She has no name. She is Everywoman."

"She's not me," Sellup retorted.

"Just so," Calap replied, and then resumed. "'Great Fenn' said she, 'you come to the camp of the Ifayle Imass, the clan of the

White Ferret. We invite you to be our guest for the time of your stay, however long you wish it to be. You shall be our brother.' She did not, as you may note, speak of the dire state of her kin. She voiced no excuse or said one word to diminish his expectation. Suffering must wait in the mist, and vanish with the sun's light, and the sun's light is found in every stranger's eyes—"

"That was stupid," said Oggle Gush, her opinion rewarded with a nod from Sellup. "If she'd said 'we're all starving,' why, then he'd go away."

"If that happened," said Apto Canavalian, "there can be no story, can there?"

"Sure there can! Tell us what she's wearing! I want to know every detail and how she braids her hair and the paints she uses on her face and nipples. And I want to hear how she's in charge of everything and secretly smarter than everyone else, because that's what heroes are, smarter than everyone else. They see clearest of all! They wear Truth and Honour—isn't that what you always say, Nifty?"

The man coughed and looked uncomfortable. "Well, not precisely. That is, I mean—what I meant is, well, complicated. That's what I meant. Now, let Calap continue, I pray you, darling."

"What do they look like?" Apto asked Oggle.

"What does what look like?"

"Truth and Honour. Is Truth, oh, fur-trimmed? Line stitched? Brocaded? And what about Honour? Do you wear Honour on your feet? Well tanned? Softened with worn teeth and the gums of old women?"

"You do maybe," Oggle retorted, "wear them, I mean," and then she rolled her eyes and said, "Idiot."

Calap continued, "To her words the Fenn warrior did bow, and together they walked to the circle of round-tents, where the chill winds rushed through the furs of the stretched hides. Three hunters were present, two men and another woman, and they came out to greet the stranger. They knew he would have words to speak, and they knew, as well, that he would only speak them before the fire of the chief's hut. In good times, the arrival of a stranger leads to delight and excitement, and all, be they children or elders, yearn to hear tales of doings beyond their selves, and such tales are of course the currency a stranger pays for the hospitality of the camp."

"Just as a modern bard travels from place to place," commented Apto. "Poets, each of you can lay claim to an ancient tradition—"

"And for reward you kill and eat us!" snapped Brash Phluster. "Those horses—"

"Will not be sacrificed," uttered Tulgord Vise, in a low growl of lifted hackles. "That was settled and so it remains."

Tiny Chanter laughed with a show of his tiny teeth and said to Tulgord, "When we done ate all the artists, peacock, it's you or your horses. Take your pick." His brothers laughed too and their laughs were the same as Tiny's, and at this moment the knights exchanged glances and then both looked to Steck Marynd who rode a few paces ahead, but the forester's back stayed hunched and if his hairs prickled on his neck he made no sign.

Tiny's threat remained, hanging like a raped woman's blouse

that none would look at, though Brash seemed pleased by it, evidently not yet thinking through Tiny's words.

"The Chief in the camp was past his hunting years, and wisdom made bleak his eyes, for when word came to him that a Fenn had made entrance, and that he brought with him a sled on which lay a body, the Chief feared the worst. There was scant food, and the only medicines the shoulder-women still possessed—after such trying months—were those that eased hunger pangs. Yet he made welcome his round floor and soon all those still able to walk had gathered to meet the Fenn and to hear his words."

Clearing his throat, Calap resumed. "The woman who had first greeted him, fair as the spring earth, could not but feel responsible for his presence—though she was bound to honour and so had had no choice—and so she walked close by him and stood upon his left as they waited for the Chief's invitation to sit. Soft the strange whisperings within her, however, and these drew her yet closer, as if his need was hers, as if his straits simply awaited the strength of her own shoulders. She could not explain such feeling, and knew then that the spirits of her people had gathered close to this moment, beneath grey and lifeless skies, and the strokes upon her heart belonged to them.

"It is fell and frightening when the spirits crowd the realm of mortals, for purposes remain ever hidden and all will is as walls of sand before the tide's creep. So, fast beat her heart, quickening her breath, and when at last a child emerged from his grandfather's hut and gestured, she reached out and took hold of the stranger's hand—her own like a babe's within it, and feeling too the hard calluses and seams of strength—and he in turn looked with hooded surprise down upon her, seeing for the very first time her youth, her wan beauty, and something like pain flinched in his heavy eyes—"

"Why?" Sellup asked. "What does he know?"

"Unwelcome your chorus," muttered Apto Canavalian.

Calap rubbed his face, as if in sudden loss. Had he forgotten the next details? Did the Reaver now stand before him, Death at home in his camp?

"Before the fire . . ." said I in soft murmur.

Starting, Calap nodded. "Before the fire, and with the sled left outside where the last of the dogs drew close to sniff and dip tails, the Fenn warrior made sit before the Chief. His weapons were left at the threshold, and in the heat he at last drew free of his wintry clothing, revealing a face in cast not much elder to the woman kneeling beside him. Blood and suffering are all-too-common masks among all people throughout every age. In dreams we see the hale and fortunate and imagine them some other place, yet one within reach, if only in aspiration. Closer to our lives, waking each day, we must face the scarred reality, and all too often we don our own matching masks, when bereft of privilege as most of us are." It seemed he faltered then, as if the substance of this last aside now struck him for the first time.

Statements find meaning only in the extremity of the witness, else all falls flat and devoid of emotion, and no amount of authorial exhortation can awaken sincerity among those crouch'd in strongholds of insensitivity. No poorer luck seeking to stir dead soil to life, no seed will take, no flower will grow. True indeed the dead poet's young vision of masks of suffering and blood, but true as well—as he might have seen in his last days and nights—a growing plethora of masks of the insensate, the dead-inside, the fallow of soul, who are forever beyond reach.

Calap cleared his throat yet again. "The Chief was silent and patient. Tales will wait. First, meagre staples are shared, for to eat in company is to acknowledge the kinship of need and, indeed, of pleasure no matter how modest." And once more he hesitated, and we all walked silent and brittle of repose.

"Too grim," announced Tiny. "Brash Phluster, weave us another song and be quick about it."

Calap staggered and would have fallen if not for my arm.

Brash weaved as if punched and suddenly sickly his pallor. Drawing deep, ragged breaths, he looked round wildly, as if seeking succor, but no eyes but mine would meet his and as he fixed his terror upon me I inclined my head and gave him the strength of my assurance.

Gulping, he tried out his singing voice. "Va la gla blah! Mmmmmmm. Himmyhimmyhimmy!"

Behind us the harashal vulture answered in kind, giving proof to the sordid rumour of the bird's talent at mimicry.

"Today," Brash began in a reedy, quavering voice, "I shall sing my own reworking of an ancient poem, a chapter of the famous epic by Fisher kel Tath, *Anomandaris*."

Apto choked on something and the host ably pounded upon his back until the spasm passed.

One of the mules managed a sharp bite of Flea's left shoulder and he bellowed in pain, lumbering clear. The other mule laughed as mules were in the habit of doing. The Chanters as one wheeled to glare at Mister Ambertroshin, who shook his head and said, "Flea slowed his steps, he did. The beasts are hungry, aye?"

Tulgord Vise turned at that. "You, driver," he barked, "from where do you hail?"

"Me, sir? Why, Theft that'd be. A long way away, aye, no argument there, and varied the tale t'bring me here. A wife, you see, and plenty of Oponn's infernal pushings. Should we run outta tales, why, I could spin us a night or two."

"Indeed," the Mortal Sword replied dryly, one gauntleted hand settling on his sword's shiny pommel, but this gesture was solitary as he once more faced forward in the saddle.

"For your life?" Arpo Relent asked, rather bitingly.

Mister Ambertroshin's bushy brows lifted. "I'd sore your stomach something awful, good sir. Might well sicken and kill you at that. Besides, the Dantoc Calmpositis, being a powerful woman rumoured to be skilled in the sorcerous arts, why, she'd be most displeased at losing her servant, I dare say."

The host gaped at that and then said, "Sorcerous? The Dantoc? I'd not heard—"

"Rumours only, I'm sure," Mister Ambertroshin said, and he smiled round his pipe.

"What does 'Dantoc' mean?" Arpo demanded.

"No idea," the driver replied.

"What?"

"It's just a title, ain't it? Some kind of title. I imagine." He shrugged. "Sounds like one, t'me that is, but then, being a foreigner to it all, I can't really say either way."

A tad wildly, Arpo Relent looked round. "Anyone?" he

demanded. "Anyone heard that title before? You, Apto, you're from here, aren't you? What's a 'Dantoc'?"

"Not sure," the Judge admitted. "I don't pay much attention to such things, I'm afraid. She's well known enough in the city, to be sure, and indeed highly respected and possibly even feared. Her wealth has come from slave trading, I gather."

"Anomandaris!" Brash shrieked, startling all three horses (but not the mules).

"*Anomandaris!*" cried the vulture, startling everyone else (but not the mules).

"Right," said Tiny, "get on with it, Phluster."

"I shall! Hark well and listen to hear my fair words! This song recounts the penultimate chapter of the Slaying of Draconus—"

"You mean 'ultimate' surely," said Apto Canavalian.

"What?"

"Please, Brash, forgive my interruption. Do proceed."

"The Slaying of Draconus, and so . . ."

He cleared his throat, assumed that peculiar mask of performance that seemed to afflict most poets, and then fell into that stentorian cadence they presumably all learned from each other and from generations past. Of what stentorian cadence do I speak? Why, the one that seeks to import meaning and significance to every damned word, of course, even when no such resonance obtains. After all, is there really anything more irritating (and somnolent) than a poetry reading?

> "*Dark was the room*
> *Deep was the gloom*
> *That was Draconus's tomb*

Dank was the air
Daunting the bier
On which he laid eyes astare

The chains not yet broken
For he not yet woken
His vows not yet revoken
His sword still to awaken
In its scabbard black oaken
Cold hands soon to stroken"

"Gods below, Phluster!" snarled Calap Roud. "The original ain't slave to rhymes, and those ones are awful! Just sing it as Fisher would and spare us all your version!"

"You're just jealous! I'm making Fisher's version accessible to everyone, even children! That's the whole point!"

"It's a tale of betrayal, incest and murder, what are on earth are you doing singing it to children?"

"It's only the old who get shocked these days, old man!"

"And it's no wonder, with idiots like you singing to innocent children!"

"Got to keep them interested, Calap, something you never did understand, even with a grown-up audience! Now, be quiet and keep your opinions to yourself, I got a song to sing!

"And his head flew into the air
On a fountain of gore and hair!
And—"

"Hold on, poet," said Tiny, "I think you missed a verse there."

"What? Oh, damn! Wait."

"And it better start getting funny, too."

"Funny? But it's not a funny story!"

"I get his brain," said Midge. "All that fat."

"You get half," said Flea.

"Wait! Here, here, wait—

"Envy and Spite were the daughters
To the Consort of Dark Fathers
She the left breast and her the right
Two tits named Envy and Spite!
And deadly their regarrrrd!
Cold the nipples' rewarrrrd!
And when Anomander rose tall
Between them so did they fall
Sliding down in smears of desire
Down the bold warrior's gleaming spire!
And crowded the closet!
Sharp the cleaving hatchet!"

"Damn me, poet," said Tulgord Vise, "the Tomb of Draconus has a closet?"

"They had to hide somewhere!"

"From what, a dead man?"

"He was only sleeping—"

"Who sleeps in a tomb? Was he ensorcelled? Cursed?"

"He ate a poisoned egg," suggested Nifty Gum, "which was

secreted into the clutch of eggs he was served for breakfast. There was a wicked witch who haunted the secret passages of the rabbit hole behind the carrot patch behind the castle—"

"I hate carrots," said Flea.

Brash Phluster was tearing at his hair. "What castle? It was a tomb I tell you! Even Fisher agrees with me!"

"A carrot through the eye can kill as easily as a knife," observed Midge.

"I hate witches, too," said Flea.

"I don't recall any hatchet in Anomandaris," said Apto Canavalian. "Rake had a sword—"

"And we been hearing all about it," said Relish Chanter, and was too bold in her wink at me, but for my fortune none of her brothers were paying any attention to her.

"I don't recall much sex either—and you're singing your version to children, Brash? Gods, there must be limits."

"On art? Never!" cried Brash Phluster.

"I want to hear about the poisoned egg and the witch," said Sellup.

Nifty Gum smiled. "The witch had a terrible husband who spoke the language of the beasts and knew nothing of humankind, and in seeking to teach him the gifts of love the witch failed and was cast aside. Spiteful and bitter, she pronounced a vow to slay every man upon the world, at least, all those who were particularly hairy. Those she could not kill she would seduce only to shave clean their chest and so steal their power, which she stored in the well at the top of the hill. But her husband of old haunted her still, and at night she dreamed of warped mirrors bearing both her face and his and sometimes the two were one in the same.

"The city was named Tomb. This detail, by the way, is what confused legions of artists, including Fisher himself, who, dare I add, is not so nearly as tall as me. And Draconus was the city's king, a proud and noble ruler. Indeed he had two daughters, born of no mother, but of his will and magic gifts. Shaped of clay and sharp stones, neither possessed a heart. Their names they took upon themselves the night they became women, when each saw her own soul's truth and could not look away, could not lie or deceive even unto their own selves."

Noting at last the host of blank expressions, he said, "The significance of this—"

"Is a form of torture I will not abide," said Tiny Chanter.

"Carrot through the eye," said Midge. "Anyone got a carrot?"

"Eye," said Flea.

"Anomander kills Draconus and gets the sword!" shouted Brash Phluster. "You never let me get to the funny bits—you can't vote, it's not fair!"

"Oh be quiet, will you?" said Tulgord Vise. "Plenty of light left this day, and we've plenty of cooked meat from yesterday. No, what we need is water. Sardic Thew, what chance the next spring is dry?"

The host stroked his jaw. "We've no more than trickles for days now, in every watering hole. I admit I am worried mightily, good sir."

"Might have to bleed someone," said Tiny, showing his tiny teeth again. "Who's flush?"

His brothers laughed.

I spoke then. "Vows are as stone, each a menhir raised like a knuckled finger to the sky. The knights who hunted the Nehemoth were not alone in such cold chisel. Another traveled in the group, a strange and silent man who walked like a hunter in forestlands, yet in his face could be seen the ragged scrawl of a soldier's cruel life, a past of friends dying in his arms, of the guilt of surviving, of teeth bared to fickle chance and a world stripped of all meaning. The gods are as nothing to a soldier, who in prayer only begs for life and righteous purpose, and both are selfish needs indeed. This is not reaching up to touch god. It is pulling the god down as if stealing a golden idol upon a mantelpiece. Begging voiced as a demand, a plea paid out as if owed, such are a soldier's prayers.

"Faith fell beneath his marching boots long ago. He knows the curse of reconciliation and knows too its falsity, the emptiness of the ritual. He has abandoned redemption and now lives to excoriate a stain from the world. That stain being the Nehemoth. In this, perhaps, he is the noblest of them all—"

"Not true!" hissed Arpo Relent. "The Well Knight serves only the Good, the Wellness of the soul and the flesh that is its home! Not a single three-finned fish has ever passed these lips! Not a sip of wretched liquor, not a stream of noxious smoke. Vegetables are the gift of god—"

"Didn't stop you stuffing your maw last night though, did it?"

Arpo glared at Tiny who grinned back. "Necessity—"

"Of which the hunter and soldier understood all too well," I resumed. "Necessity indeed. The vow stands tall upon the horizon, bold in bleak skies. Even the sun's light cringes from that dark stone. Has rock earned worship? Does a man so lose himself as to kneel before insensate stone? Does one cherish home or the walls and ceiling so enclosing? To see that vow each day, each night, season upon season, year upon year, is it any wonder that it becomes unto itself a god before the supplicant's eyes? In making vows we chisel the visage of a master and announce our abjection as its slave.

"Yet, does not the soldier now standing unmoving behind his eyes not see and understand the dissembling demanded of him, the bending of reason, the burnishing into blindness the madness of absurd conviction? He does, and is mocked within himself, and the god of his vow is a closed fist inside iron scales and those iron scales mark the lie of his own hand, there upon the saddle horn."

At last, Steck Marynd did twist round in his saddle. "You presume at your peril, poet."

"As do we all," I replied. "I tell but a tale here. The hunter's face is not your face. The knights are not as travel here in our company. The carriage is nothing like the carriage in my tale. To noble Purse Snippet I paint a scene close enough to be familiar, indeed, comfortable, as much as such luxury can be achieved here on this fatal trail."

"Rubbish," said Steck. "You steal from what you see and claim it invention."

"Indeed, by simple virtue of changing a name or two here and there, or perhaps it is enough to say that what I relate is not what you may see around you. Each listener crowds eager with an armful of details and shall fill in and buttress up as he or she sees fit."

Apto Canavalian was frowning, as Judges are in the habit of doing when they can't really think of anything worth thinking. He then shook his head, casting off the momentary fug, and said, "I see no real value in changing a few names and then making everyone pretend it isn't what it obviously is. How is this invention, or even creative? Where is the imagination?"

"Buried six feet down, I should think," said I, and smiled. "In some far off land in no way similar to any place you know, of course."

"Then why bother with the pathetic shell-game, now you've shown us where the nut hides?"

"Did I really need to show you for you to know where it is?"

"No, which makes it even more ridiculous."

"I most heartily agree, sir," said I. "Now, if you will permit, may I continue?"

Flitting eagerness in the Judge's eyes, as if at last he understood. It warms the soul when this is witnessed, I do assure you.

Before I could speak, however, Purse Snippet asked, "Poet, how fares their trek, these hunters and pilgrims of yours?"

"Not well. In flesh and in spirit, they are all lost. The enemy has drawn close—closer than any among them is aware—"

"What!" bellowed Tulgord Vise, wheeling his horse around and half-drawing his sword. "Do you glean too close to a secret here, Flicker? Dare not be coy with me. I kill coy people out of faint irritation, and you venture far beyond that! You sting like spider hairs in the eye! On your life, speak true!"

"Not once have I strayed from what is true, sir. Now you show us your clutter of details and would build us something monstrous! Shall I weigh upon your effort? Terrible its flaws, sir, set no hope or belief upon such a rickety frame. This tale is thin and clear as a mountain rook. Sir, the blinding mud so stirred resides behind your eyes and nowhere else."

"You dare insult me?"

"Not at all. But may I remind you, my life is in the palm of Lady Snippet, not in yours, sir. And I am telling her a tale, and for this breath at least she withholds her judgement on its merit. In the Lady's name, may I continue?"

"What's all this?" Tiny demanded. "Flea?"

Flea scowled.

"Midge?"

Midge scowled, too.

The host waved his hands. "Whilst you slept—"

"While we sleep everything stops!" Tiny roared, his face the hue of masticated roses. "No votes! No decisions! No nothing!"

"Incorrect," said Purse Snippet, and so flat and so certain her tone that the Chanters were struck dumb. "I am not chained to you," she went on, her eyes knuckling hard as stone upon Tiny's faltering visage. "And the blades with which you would seek to threaten me strike no fear in this breast. I have charged this poet to speak me a story, to continue what I so poorly began. If he fails in satisfying me, he dies. This is the pact and it does not concern you, nor anyone else here. Only myself and Avas Flicker."

"And how does he fair so far, Milady?" Apto asked.

"Poorly," she said, "but for the moment I shall abide."

. . .

The day was most desultory, in the manner of interminable treks the world over. Heat oppressed, the ground grew harder underfoot, stones sharp stabbed beneath soles already tender with threat. The ancient pilgrim track was rutted and dusty, repository of every discarded or surrendered aspiration and ambition. To journey is to purge, as all wise ancients know, and of purging the elderly know better than most.

But what burdens could be so cast off our straining shoulders here on Cracked Pot Trail? Crushing and benumbing this weight, that our art should have purpose, but dare I hazard that those of you who are witness to this grim tale who are neither poet nor musician, not sculptor or painter, you cannot hope to imagine the sudden prickling sweat that bespeaks performance, no matter its shaping. Within the heated skull vicious thoughts ravage the softer allowances. *What if my audience is composed of nothing but idiots? Raving lunatics! What if their tastes are so bad not even a starving vulture would pluck loose a single rolling eyeball? What if they hate me on sight? Look at all those faces! What do they see and what notions ply the unseen waters of their thoughts? Am I too fat, too thin, too nervous, too ugly to warrant all this attention?* The composing of art is the most private of endeavours, but the performance paints the face in most dramatic hues. Does failure in one devour the other? *Do I even like any of these people? What do they want with me anyway? What if—what if I just ran away? No! They'd hate me even more than they do now! Dare I speak out?* Ah, these are most unwelcome streams, swirling so dark and biting. Assume the best and let the worst arrive as revelation (and, perhaps, dismay). An artist truly contemptuous of his or her audience deserves nothing but contempt in return.

But, the razor voice inside softly whispers, *idiots abound.*

No matter. The rocky outcrops are patiently ticking, the blue sky egalitarian in its indifference, the sun unmindful of all who would challenge its stare. The story belongs to the selfsame world, implacable as stone, resistant to all pressures, be they breath's wind or rain's piss. The mules plod befuddled by their own weight and clopping strain. The heads of the horses droop and nod, tails flicking to keep the flies alert. The plateau stretches on into grainy white haze.

"I am not happy about this," Tiny said in pique, his girthless eyes flitting. "Special rules and all that. Once special rules start, everything falls apart."

"Listen to the thug," Arpo Relent said.

"Midge?"

Midge spat and said, "Tiny Chanter is head of the Chanters, and the Chanters rule Toll's City of Stratem. We chased out the Crimson Guard to do it, too. Tiny's a king, you fool."

"If he's a king," Arpo retorted, "what's he doing here? Stratem? Never heard of Stratem. Crimson Guard? Who're they?"

Calap said, "Since when does a king wander around without bodyguards and servants and whatnot? It's a little hard to believe, your claim."

"Flea?"

Flea scratched in his beard and looked thoughtful. "Well, me and Midge and Relish, we're the bodyguards, but we ain't servants. King Tiny don't need servants and such. He's a sorceror, you see. And the best fighter in all Stratem."

"What kind of sorceror?" the host demanded.

"Midge?"

"He can raise the dead. That kind of sorceror."

At that the pace stumbled to a halt, and Steck Marynd reined in to slowly swing his horse round, the crossbow cradled in one arm. "Necromancer," he said, baring his teeth and it was not a smile. "So what makes you any different from the Nehemoth? That is what I want to know."

Midge and Flea stepped out to the sides, hands settling on the grips of their weapons as Tulgord Vise drew his sister-blessed sword and Arpo Relent looked around confusedly. Tiny grinned. "The difference? Ain't nobody hunting me, that's the *difference.*"

"The only one?" Steck asked in a dull tone.

Was it alarm that flickered momentarily in Tiny's eyes? Too difficult to know for certain. "Eager to die, are you, Marynd? I can kill you without raising a finger. Just a nod and your guts would be spilling all over your saddle horn." He looked around, his grin stretching. "I'm the deadliest person here, best you all understand that."

"You're bluffing," said Tulgord. "Dare you challenge the Mortal Sword of the Sisters, oaf?"

Tiny snorted. "As if the Sisters care a whit about the Nehemoth—a madman and a eunuch never destroyed the world or toppled a god. Them two are irritants and nothing more. If you truly was the Sisters' Mortal Sword, they must be pretty annoyed by now. You running all over every damned continent and what for? An insult? That's what it was, wasn't it? They made a fool of you, and you'll burn down half the world all because of wounded pride."

Tulgord Vise was a most frightening hue of scarlet wherever skin was visible. He stepped forward. "And you, Chanter?" he retorted amidst gnashing teeth. "Hunting down a pair of rivals? I agree with Steck, necromancers are an abomination, and you are necromancer. Therefore, you are—"

"An abomination!" shrieked Arpo Relent, fumbling with his axe.

"Midge, pick one."

"That girl there, the one with only one eyebrow."

Tiny nodded. He gestured slightly with his left hand.

Sellup seemed to vomit something even as she pitched forward, limbs rattling on the sand before falling still. Face down on the ground, motionless in death, and all eyes upon her. Eyes that then widened.

"Beru bless us!" moaned the host.

Sellup moved, lifted to her hands and knees, her hair hanging down and clotted with—what was it, blood? She raised her head. Her visage was lifeless, the eyes dull with death, her mouth slack in the manner of the witless and fanatic fans of dubious sports. "Who killed me?" she asked in a grating voice, tongue protruding like a drowning slug. A strange groaning noise from her nose announced the escape of the last air to grace her lungs. "That wasn't fair. There was no cause. Pampera, is my hair a mess? Look, it's a mess. I'm a mess." She climbed to her feet, her motions clumsy and loose. "Nifty? Beloved? Nifty? I was always for you, only you."

But when she turned to him he backed away in horror.

"Not fair!" cried Sellup.

"One less mouth to feed, though," muttered Brash Phluster.

"You killed one of my fans!" Nifty Gum said, eyes like two dustbird eggs boiling in a saucer.

"It's all right," simped Oggle Gush, "you still have us, sweetthumb!"

"Tiny Chanter," said Steck Marynd, "if I see so much as a finger twitch from you again you're a dead man. We got us a problem here. Y'see, I get hired to kill necromancers—it's the only reason I'm still hunting the Nehemoth, because I guarantee satisfaction, and in my business without my word meaning something I'm nothing."

Tiny grunted. "Anybody hired you to kill me?"

"No, which is why you're still alive. But, you see, over the years, I've acquired something of a dislike for necromancers. No, that's too mild. I despise them. Loathe them, in fact."

"Too bad," said Tiny. "You only got one quarrel and you won't get a chance to re-load before one or more of us get to you. Want to die, Steck?"

"I doubt it will be as uneven as you seem to think," Steck Marynd replied. "Is that a fair thing to say, Mortal Sword?"

"It is," said Tulgord Vise in a growl.

"And you, Well Knight?"

Arpo finally had his axe ready. "Abomination!"

"This is great!" said Brash Phluster in what he likely thought was a whisper.

Tiny's tiny eyes snapped to him. "For you artists, yes it's perfect, isn't it? It was your meddling that caused all this." And with that he looked straight at me. "Devious tale—you'll spin us all to death!"

Innocent my regard. "Sire?"

"I don't know Flicker's game and I don't much care," said Steck Marynd, his stony eyes still fixed upon Tiny Chanter. "You claim to be hunting the Nehemoth. Why?"

"I don't answer to you," Tiny replied.

"You killed one of my fans!"

"I still love you, Nifty!" Arms opening, Sellup made pouting motions with her dry lips and advanced on her beloved.

He howled and ran.

Oggle shot Sellup a vicious glare. "See what you done!" she hissed, and then set off in pursuit of the Great Artist.

Pampera posed for an instant, arching to gather and sweep back her hair, her breasts pushing like a pair of seals rising for air, and then with an oddly languorous lunge she flowed into a fluid sprint, buttocks bouncing most invitingly.

> "In the wayward seas
> My love rolls in heaving swells
> Can a man drown with a smile
> Plunging deep beneath the foam?"

To my heartfelt quotation, Brash Phluster gusted a sigh and nodded. "Gormle Ess of Ivant, aye, he knew his art—"

"Sandroc of Blight," Calap Roud corrected. "Gormle Ess wrote the Adulterer's Lament." He tilted his head back and assumed the orator's posture, hands out to the sides.

> *"She was beauty beheld*
> *In shadows so sweet*
> *Where the fragrant blossoms*
> *Could kiss the tongue*
> *With honey dreams!*
> *She was desire adamant*
> *So soft to quiver under touch*
> *Leaning close in heat*
> *All this she was and more—*
> *Last night—oh the ale fumes*
> *Fail to abide the mole's squint*
> *In dread morning light!"*

"*Oh sorrow!*" cried Sellup, clapping her hands and offering everyone a bright and ghastly smile.

Arpo, staring up the trail, suddenly spoke. "Could be the coward's running . . . from us."

"We got horses," said Tulgord Vise. "They won't get away."

"Even so, we should resume our journey." Arpo then jabbed a mailed finger at Tiny. "I will be watching you, sorceror." Taking his horse's reins, he set off.

Tiny grinned at Steck Marynd. "The Well Knight has the memory of a twit-bird. Leave off, Marynd. When we finally corner the Nehemoth, you'll want me at your side. In the meantime—"

"In the meantime," Steck jerked his head at Sellup, "no more of that."

"I was only making a point," Tiny replied. "And I don't expect to have to make it twice. Midge?"

"Once will do."

"Flea?"

"Once."

The march resumed, because time yields to no reins, nor its plodding course turned aside by wishes or will. The mules cloppled, the carriage clattered, the horses snorted, and we who would claim to exception and privilege among all the things of this world, we measured each and every step in bitter humiliation. Oh, we stood taller in our minds, as is reason's hollow gift, but what do such conceits avail us in the end?

Sixty paces ahead rose the tumulus announcing the wellspring, the heap of stones fluttering with bleached rags stuffed in cracks like banners of the crushed. But of Nifty Gum and his Entourage of Two there was no sign.

Snarling under his breath, Tulgord Vise kicked his horse into a canter, riding for the spring. Dust swirled like a mummer's cape in his wake. With a click of his tongue Steck Marynd rode out to one side and stood in his stirrups, scanning the horizons.

Calap Roud and Brash Phluster drew close to me.

"This is bad, Flicker," Calap muttered with low breath. "We can maybe eat Sellup tonight, if she ain't gone foul by then."

"We should eat her now," Brash interjected. "That'd save us all for another night, wouldn't it? Wouldn't it? We got to suggest it—you do it, Flicker. Go on—"

"Good sir," said I, "I am of no mind whatsoever to suggest such a heinous thing. Tell me, would you have her complain all the while? While a single piece of her flesh exists, the curse of the unliving remains—what eternal torment would you consign to the poor lass? Besides," I added, "I know little of the art of necromancy, but it occurs to me that such flesh is itself poison to the living. Will you risk becoming an undead?"

Brash licked his lips, his face white. "Gods below!"

"What if Nifty got away?" Calap demanded. "It's impossible. He must be hiding out there somewhere. Him and his women. His kind get all the luck! Think of it, he's got an undying fan! I'd kill for that!"

"Calap Roud," said I, "your tale of the Imass is cause for concern. Where it leads . . ."

"But it's all I got, Flicker! The only one I remember word for word—"

"Hold on!" said Brash. "It ain't yours? That's cheating!"

"No it isn't. Nobody said it had to be our own compositions. This isn't the Festival. They just want to be entertained, so if you need to steal then steal! Gods, listen to me. I'm giving you advice! My rival. Both of you! Flicker, listen! It's your story that's going to get us all killed. You're too close to what's really going on here—"

"Am I? I think not, sir. Besides, my task now is quite different from the one you two face."

"That was some fancy trickery from you, too! She knows we

can do a day or three without food. She only has to make sure you outlive me and Phluster, and then you can make the last long run to the ferry landing. You're in cahoots, and don't deny it!"

Brash Phluster smirked. "It don't matter, Roud, because Flicker's going to lose. And soon, before either of us."

Arch did an eyebrow upon my benign demeanor. "Indeed?"

"Indeed," he mimicked, wagging his head. "You see, I saw you, last night. And I saw her, too."

Calap gasped. "He's rollicking Purse Snippet? I knew it!"

"Not her," Brash said, his eyes bright upon me, "Relish Chanter. I seen it, and if I tell Tiny—and maybe I'll have to, to buy my life, why, you're a dead man, Flicker."

Calap was suddenly grinning. "We got him. We got Flicker. Hah! We're safe, Brash! You and me, we're going to make it!"

Did I quiver in terror? Did my knees rattle and bladder loosen to the prickly bloom of mortal panic? Did I fling myself at Brash, hands closing about his scrawny throat? An elbow to the side of Calap's head? Did my mind race, seeking an escape? "Good sirs, more of this discussion anon. We have reached the spring."

"Aye," said Calap, "we can wait, can't we, Brash?"

But Phluster grasped my arm. "Your tale's going to go sour, Flicker. I know, you was nice to me but it's too late for that kind of stuff. You were only generous because you felt safe. I'm not such a fool as to take such patronization from one such as you! I *am* a genius! You're going to disappoint Snippet, do you understand me?"

"I shall resume my tale, then, once we have slaked our thirsts."

Brash's grin broadened.

"I always hated you," said Calap, now studying me as he would a worm. "Did you know that, Flicker? Oh, I saw the aplomb in your pertinence, and knew it as a fraud from the very first! Always acting like you knew a secret nobody else knows. And that smile you show every now and then—it makes me sick. Do you still think it's all so amusing? Do you? Besides, your tale's stupid. It can't go anywhere, can it, because what you're stealing from isn't done yet, is it? You're doomed to just repeat what's already happened and they won't take that much longer. So, even without Phluster's ultimatum, you're doomed to lose. You'll die. We'll carve you up and eat you, and we'll feel good about it, too!"

Ah, artists! "The truth of the tale," said I, most calmly, "is not where it is going, but where it has been. Ponder that, if you've the energy. In the meantime, sustenance beckons, for I see that some water survives still, and Mister Must is already unhitching the mules. Best we drink before the beasts do, yes?"

Both men pushed past me in their haste.

I followed at a more leisurely pace. I have this thing, you see, about anticipation and abnegation, but of that, later.

Steck had ridden up and was now dismounting. "Found their tracks," he said, presumably to Tulgord. "As we know they must stay relatively close to the trail, however, we need not worry overmuch. Deprivation will bring them back."

"We can go hunting, too," said Tiny. "A bit of excitement," and he smiled his tiny ratty smile.

"Drink your fill," cried the host, "all of you! Such benison! The gods have mercy, yes they do! Oh, perhaps this will suffice!

Perhaps we can complete our journey without the loss of another life! I do implore you all, sirs! We can—"

"We eat the artists," rumbled Tiny. "It was decided and there ain't no point in going back on it. Besides, I've acquired a liking for the taste." And he laughed.

Midge laughed too.

So did Flea.

Relish yawned.

"We rest here," announced Steck Marynd, "for a time."

Purse Snippet was crouched down at the murky pool, splashing her face. I squatted beside her. "Sweet nectar," murmured I, reaching down.

"They're tyrants one and all," she said under her breath. "Even Steck Marynd, for all his airs."

Cool water closed about my hand with a goddess touch. "Milady, it is the nature of such paragons of virtue, but can we truly claim to anything nobler? Human flesh has passed our lips, after all."

She hissed in frustration. "Our reward for cowardly obedience!"

"Just so."

"Where will your tale lead us, poet?"

"The answer to that must, alas, wait."

"You're all the same."

"Perhaps," I ventured, "while we may taste the same, we are in taste anything but the same. So one hopes."

"You jest even now, Avas Didion Flicker? Will we ever see your true self, I wonder?"

Cupping water, I took a sip. "We shall see, Milady."

A woman I once knew possessed a Kanese Ratter, a hairy and puny lapdog with all sanity bred out of it, and hers was more crazed than most. Despite its proclivities, which included attacking in a frenzy overly loud children and stealing the toys and rattles of babies, the beast was entirely capable of standing on its hind legs for inordinate amounts of time, and its owner was most proud of this achievement. Training with tidbits and whatnot was clearly efficacious even when the subject at hand possessed a brain the size of a betel nut.

I was witness to such proof again when, at a single jab of one finger from Tiny Chanter, Calap Roud sat straight, all blood rushing from his face. Sputtering, he said, "But Flicker's volunteered—"

"Later for him. Tell us about the giant and the woman."

"But—"

"Kill him?" Midge asked.

"Kill him?" Flea asked.

"Wait! The tale, yes, the tale. Now, when we last saw them, the Fenn warrior was seated before the chief and a scant meal was being shared out. Gestures are ever delicate among such tribes. Language speaks without a single word spoken. In this song of nuance, it was understood by all the Imass that a terrible fate had befallen the warrior, that grief gripped the Fenn's broad, wounded shoulders. He bled within and without. His troubled eyes found no other in their weary wandering over the wealth of the chief, the furs and beaded hides, the shell-strung belts and steatite pipes, the circle masks with the skins of beastly faces stretched over them—the brold bear, the ay wolf, the tusked seal. Of the meagre portions of rancid blubber, dried berries and steeped moss tea, he ate each morsel with solemn care and sipped the tea with tender pleasure, but all was tinged with something bitter, a flavour stained upon his tongue—one that haunted him."

We were gathered, squatting or seated in the shade of the carriage and the stolid mules. The wellspring's basin trickled as it slowly refilled with water. Flies danced on the mud our passages had left behind. Steck Marynd had dismantled his crossbow and was cleaning each part with an oiled cloth. Midge had produced a brace of fighting knives and was making use of a large boulder bearing the grooves of past sharpening, the *whisk-whisk-whisk* sound a grating undercurrent grisly in its portent. The host, Sardic Thew, had built a small fire on which to brew tea. Brash Phluster sat leaning against one gouged carriage wheel, examining his fingernails. Purse Snippet had walked behind the carriage to prepare her small pewter cup a few moments earlier, and now sat on my left, whilst to my right was Apto Canavalian, surreptitiously sipping from a small flask every now and then. Flea and Relish had begun dozing, and Mister Must sat upon the driver's seat of the carriage, drawing upon his pipe. Arpo Relent and Tulgord Vise sat opposite each other, askance their mutually resentful glances. Thus, we were assembled to hear Calap's tale.

"The maiden, kneeling to the Fenn's right, could hear little more than the drum of her own heart. What flower this thing called love, to burst so sudden upon the colourless sward? Its seed is a ghost that even the wind carries unknowing. The blossom shouts to life, a blaze of impossible hue, and in its wild flush it summons the sun itself. So bright! So pure! She had never before known such sensations. They frightened her, stealing all control from her thoughts, from her very flesh. She felt swollen of spirit. She could feel the rough truth of his scarred arm against her own, though they did not touch. She felt herself swaying closer to him with every breath he drew into himself, only to sway back at his exhalation.

"In all things of self, she was still a child, and her soft cheeks glowed as if lit with the fire of the hearth, as if all coverings but the sky could not contain her heat. Softly, unnoticed by any, she panted, every breath shallow and making her feel half-drunk. Her eyes were black pools, the sweat swam upon her palms, and in the folds between her legs a coal fanned hot and eager.

"The flower is suffering's gift, its only gift. Did her kin see it? Did its sweet scent fill the hut? Perhaps, but the winter's cruel ways had stolen the warmth from their souls. They sat in misery, wilted with need, and as the Fenn ate all he was offered they saw the count of their days diminishing. Before their eyes, they witnessed his return to strength and hale vigour. When blood flows, the place it leaves becomes pale and weak, whilst the new home deepens rich with life. They could not shake the chill from their huddled forms, and outside the sun surrendered to the Blackhaired Witches of night, and the wind awoke with a

howl than spun long and twisted into a moan. The hide walls
rippled. Draughts stole inside and mocked the ashes that seek
naught but contented sleep."

Calap Roud licked his lips and reached for a gourd of water.
He sipped with great care, making certain he did not disturb
the settled silts, and then set the bowl back down.

The host poured tea into Snippet's cup.

"When spake the Fenn, his voice was the bundle of furs, soft
and thick, tightly bound and barely whispering of life. His words
were Imass, proof of his worldly ways despite his evident youth—
although, of course, with the Fenn age is always difficult to
determine.

"'I am the last of my people,' said he. 'Son of a great warrior
cruelly betrayed, slain by those he thought his brothers. To such
a crime, does the son not have but one answer? This, then, is my
tale. The season was cursed. The horned beasts of the mountain
passes were nowhere to be found. The Maned Sisters of the Iron
Hair had taken them away—'"

"The who?" demanded Arpo Relent.

"Thus the Fenn named the mountains of their home, good
Knight."

"Why do people have to name everything?" Arpo demanded.
"What's wrong with 'the mountains'? The river? The valley?"

"The Knight?" retorted Tiny Chanter. "Aye, why not just 'the
idiot'?"

"'The brainless ox,'" suggested Midge.

"'The Bung-Hole Licker,'" suggested Flea.

The three men snickered.

"I never licked no—"

"Hood's breath, Relent," growled Tulgord Vise. "Details are abominations with you. Stopper your trap and let him get on with it. You, Calap. No game left in the mountains, right? Let's get on with the tale. Betrayal. Vengeance, aye, that's the making of a decent story."

" 'My father," said the Fenn, "was the Keeper of the Disc, the stone wheel upon which the tribe's life was carved—its past, its present and its future. He was, therefore, a great and important man, the equivalent of chief among the Imass. He spoke with wisdom and truth. The Maned Sisters were angry with the Fenn, who had grown careless in their rituals of propitiation. A sacrifice was necessary, he explained. One life in exchange for the lives of all.

" 'The night's gathering then chose their sacrifice. My father's second son, my own brother, five years my younger. The Clan wept, as did my father, as did I. But the Wheel was certain in its telling. In our distress—' and at that moment the Fenn warrior looked up and met the Imass Chief's eyes—'in our distress, none took notice of my father's brother, my own uncle, and the hard secret unveiled in his face.

" 'There is blood and there is love. There are women who find themselves alone, and then not alone, and there is shame held within even as the belly swells. Truth revealed can rain blood. She held to herself the crime her husband's brother had committed upon her. She held it for her love for he who was her husband.

" 'But now, on this night, she felt cut in two by a ragged knife. One of her sons would die, and in her husband's eyes she

saw tears from a love fatally wounded. Too late she cast her regard upon her beloved's brother, and saw only the mask of his
indifference.'"

"Wait, I don't understand—"

"Gods below!" burst out Tiny Chanter. "The uncle raped the
mother, you fool, and the boy chosen was the beget of that!"

"The mother's uncle raped the boy? But—"

"Kill him?" Midge asked.

"Go on, Calap," Tiny commanded.

"'In the deep of night, a knife was drawn. When a brother
slays a brother, the gods are aghast. The Maned Sisters claw
through their iron hair and the earth itself shakes and trembles.
Wolves howl in shame for their bothers of the hunt. I awoke to
hard slaughter. My mother, lest she speak. My father, too. And
of my brother and uncle, why, both were gone from the camp.'"

"Vengeance!" bellowed Tiny Chanter. "No man needs a god
when vengeance stands in its stead! He hunted them down
didn't he? Tell us!"

Calap nodded. "And so the Fenn told the tale of the hunt,
how he climbed mountain passes and survived the whelp of
winter, how he lost the trail again and again, and how he wept
when he came upon the cairn bearing the frozen carcass of his
brother, half-devoured by his uncle—who had bargained with
the darkest spirits of the shadows, all to purchase his own life.
Until at last, upon a broad glacier's canted sweep, he crossed
blades with his uncle, and of that battle even a thousand words
would be too few. Beneath the cold sun, almost blinded by the
snow and ice, they fought as only giants could fight. The spirits

themselves warred, as shadows locked with honoured light, until even the Maned Sisters fell to their knees, beseeching an end."

He paused again to sip water.

"And it was light that decided the battle—the sun's flash on the son's blade, direct into the eyes of the uncle. A deft twist, a slash, and upon the crushed and broken ice and snow a crimson stream now poured, sweet as the spring's thaw.

"And so the son stood, the slayings avenged, but a bleakness was upon his soul. He was now alone in his family. He was, he knew, also the murderer of kin. And that night, as he lay sleeping, huddled in a rock shelter, the Maned Sisters visited upon him a dream. He saw himself, thin, weak, walking into the camp of his tribe. The season had broken, the terrible cold was gone from the air, and yet he saw no smoke, and no fires. He saw no one and as he drew closer he came upon bones, picked clean by foxes and here and there split open by the jaws of rock leopards, wolves and bears. And in the hut of his father he found the Wheel, split down the centre, destroyed forever more, and in his dream he knew that, in the moment his sword took the soul of his uncle, the Wheel had been sundered. Too many crimes in a single pool of blood—a curse had befallen the tribe. They had starved, they had torn one another apart in their madness. The warrior awoke, knowing he was now alone, his home was no more, and that there was a stain upon his soul than not even the gods could wash clean.

"Down from the mountains he came, a vessel emptied of love. Thus he told his tale, and the Imass keened and rocked to share his grief. He would stay for a time, he said, but not overlong, knowing well the burden he presented. And that night—"

"That will do," pronounced Tiny, grunting as he climbed to his feet. "Now we walk."

"It's Flicker's turn now, isn't it?" So demanded Brash Phluster.

"Not yet."

"But soon?"

"Soon." He paused and smiled. "Then we vote."

Strips of charred meat were apportioned out, skins filled one last time, the mules and horses brought close to drink again, and then the trek resumed. Chewing with an array of curious and disparate expressions, we trudged along the worn trail.

What fate had befallen this region? Why, nothing but the usual vagary. Droughts settled like a plague upon lands. Crops withered and blew away, people and beasts either died or moved on. But the track where walked pilgrims asserted something more permanent, immortal even, for belief is the blood's unbroken thread. Generation upon generation, twisted and knotted, stretched and shredded, will and desire set the cobble stones upon this harrowed road, and each is polished by sweat and suffering, hope and cherished dreams. Does enlightenment appear only upon the shadeless travail, on a frame of soured muscles and aching bones? Is blessing born solely from ordeal and deprivation?

The land trembles to the slightest footfall, the beetle and the bhederin, and in the charms of the wind one can hear countless cries for succor.

Of course, with all the chewing and gnawing going on, not one of us could hear a damned thing.

We are pilgrims of necessity, stumbling in the habits of privation.

"The Dantoc must have known a mighty thirst." So said Apto Canavalian. "Two heavy skins, just for an old woman hiding in the cool gloom."

"Elderly as she is," replied Mister Must from atop the carriage, "the Dantoc Calmpositis holds to the teaching of Mendic Hellup, whose central tenet is that water is the secret of all life, and much physical suffering comes from a chronic undernourishment of water in our bodies." He chewed on his pipe stem for a moment, and then said, "Or something like that."

"You're an odd one," Apto noted, squinting up at the driver. "Times you sound rolled up as a scholar, but others like a herder who sleeps under his cow."

"Disparate my learnings, sir."

Moments of malice come to us all. How to explain them? One might set hands upon breast and claim the righteous stance of self-preservation. Is this enough to cleanse the terrible bright splashes stinging the eye? Or what of simple instinctive retaliation from a kneeling position, bearing one's own dark wounds of flesh and spirit? A life lived is a life of regrets, and who can stand at the close of one's years and deny the twisted skeins skirled out in one's wake?

In this moment, as the burden of the tale was set upon me once more, could I have held up before my own visage a silvered mirror, would I recoil before a mien of vicious spite? Were all witness to something bestial, akin to a rock-ape's mad gleam upon discovering a bloated tick dangling from an armpit? Did I snarl like a hyena in a laughing pit? A sex-sodden woman with penis and knife in hand, or breasts descending as weapons of suffocation upon a helpless, exhausted face? Wicked my regard?

Or naught but a sleepy blink and the coolness of a trickling rill only moments from a poisonous chuckle? Pray, you decide.

"The mortal brain," quoth I, "is an amorous quagmire. Man and woman both swim sordid currents in the gurgling caverns of unfettered desire. We spread the legs of unknown women at a glance, or take possession of the Gila Monster's stubby tail in a single flutter of sultry lashes. Coy is our silent ravishing, abulge with mutual lust pungent as a drunkard's breath. In the minds of each and every one of us, bodies writhe slick with oiled perfumes, scenes flash hot as fire, and the world beyond is stripped naked to our secret eyes. We rock and we pitch, we sink fast and grasp tight. Our mouths are teased open and tongues find bedmates. Aftermaths wash away and with them all consequence, leaving only the knowing meet of eyes or that shiver of nearness with unspoken truths sweet as a lick."

None interrupted, proof of the truth of my words, and each and all had slid into and far down the wet channel so warm, so perfect in base pleasure. Sweat beaded beneath napes, walks stiffened awkward. Do you deny? What man would not roger nine of ten women he might see in a single day? Ninety of a hundred? What woman does not imagine clutching a dozen crotches and by magic touch make hard what was soft, huge what was puny? Does she not, with a shudder, then dream the draining weakness of utter surrender? We are rutters of the mind and in the array of each and every pose can be found all the misery and joy of existence. History's tumult is the travail of frustration and desire, murder the slaughter of rivals, slaying the coined purse of the spurned. Children die . . . to make room for more children! Pregnant women swing wild their trophies of conquest pitched so fierce upon their creaking hips. Young men lock horns in swagger and brainless gnashing of eyes. Old men drool over lost youth when all was possible and so little was grasped. Old women perch light as ragged songbirds on brawny young arms not even hinting of blemishes to come. But do not decry such truths! They are the glory of life itself! Make wild all celebration!

Just be sure to invite me along.

"Among the pilgrims," so I did resume after an appropriate duration to stir the stew, "maelstroms raged in silent touch of glance and hungers were awakened and the conviction of terrible starvation sizzled with certainty, and for all the threats spoken and unspoken, ah, love will find a way. Legs yearn to yawn, thighs quiver to clamp hard. Snakes strain to bludgeon into ruin all barriers to sentinel readiness.

"There was a woman," and if possible, why, even the mules and horses trod more softly to challenge not my words, "a sister to three bold warriors, and desired by all other men in the company. Hard and certain the warnings issued by the brothers.

War in answer to despoiling, a thousand legions upon the march, a siege of a hundred years and a hundred great heroes dead on the sand. The toppling of kings and wizards upon the rack. Heads on spikes and wives raped and children sold into slavery. The aghast regard of horrified gods. No less to any and all of these the stern threats from the brothers.

"But who could deny her beauty? And who could ignore the hooked bait in the net she daily cast so wide into her path and wake both?"

Did I risk a glance at Relish Chanter? I did not. But let us imagine now her precious expression at this moment. Eyes wide in horror? Lips slack? A rising flush? Or, and with surety I would cast my coin here, an odd brightness to her gaze, the hint of a half-smile, a touch wilder and wider the sway of her petalled hips. Perhaps even a deflagrant toss of her head. No young woman, after all, can be chained to childhood and all its per-verse innocence, no matter how many belligerent brothers she has in tow. The flush apple beckons every hand, and the fruit in turn yearns to be plucked.

"Among the poets and bards," said I then, "there was a states-man of the tender arts, elder in his years, but creativity's flower (still so lush in his mind) proclaimed with blind lie a vigour long past. And one night, after days of effort growing ever more desperate, ever more careless, did he finally catch the maiden's eye. Whilst the brothers slept, heads anod and snores asnore, out they crept into the night—"

"But I—"

Poor Calap Roud, alas, got no further.

With a roar, Tiny Chanter lunged upon the hapless old man.

The fist that struck the poet was driven hard as a mace, crushing visage and sending shards of bone deep into Calap's brain. In his collapse not a finger's breadth of his body evinced the remotest sign of life.

Oh dear.

Do the gods stand in wait for each and every one of us? So many do believe. Someone has to pay for this mess. But who among us does not also believe that he or she would boldly meet such immortal regard? Did we not drag our sack of excuses all this way? Our riotous justifications? Even death itself could not defy this baggage train chained to our ankles and various other protuberances. Truly, can anyone here honestly assert they would do other than argue their case, all their cases, that mountain heap of cases that is the toll of a life furtively lived?

"Yes, oh Great Ones, such was my laziness that I could not be bothered to dispose of my litter in the proper receptacles, and a thousand times I pissed against a wall behind my neighbour's house, even as I coveted and eventually seduced his wife. And yes, I was in the habit of riding my horse through town and country too quickly, exercising arrogant disregard for courtesy and caution. I cut off other riders out of spite, I threatened to trample pedestrians at every turn! I always bought the biggest horse to better intimidate others and to offset my sexual incapacities! I bullied and lied and cheated and had good reasons every time. I long ago decided that I was the centre of all exis-

tence, emperor of emperors—all this to hide my venal, pathetic self. After all, we are stupider than we like to believe: why, this is the very meaning of sentience, and if you gods are not to blame for your own miserable creations, then who is?"

Just so.

And, as poor Calap Roud's corpse cooled there on the hard ground, and all the others stared in array of horror, shock, sudden appetite, or mulish indifference, first upon Calap and then upon me, and then back again, deft in swivel to avoid the Chanters with their gnarly fists and black expressions (and Relish, of course, who stood examining her fingernails).

Yet t'was Relish who spoke first. "As if."

Extraordinary indeed, how two tiny words could shift the world about-face, the volumes of disdain and disgust, disbelief and a hundred other disses, so filling her breath by way of tone and pitch as to leave not a single witness in doubt of her veracity. Calap Roud in Relish's arms? The absurdity of that notion was as a lightning strike to blast away idiotic conviction, and in the vacuous echo of her comment, why, all eyes now fixed in outrage upon Tiny Chanter.

Whose scowl deepened. "What?"

"Now we'll never hear what happened to the Imass!" So cried our amiable host, as hosts must by nature be ever practical.

The mood soured then, until I humbly said, "Not necessarily. I know that particular tale. Perhaps not with the perfect recall with which Calap Roud iterated it, but I shall do my best to satisfy."

"Better choice than your own story," muttered Apto, "which is liable to see us all killed before you're done with it."

"Unacceptable," pronounced Purse Snippet. "Flicker owes me his tale."

"Now he owes us another one!" barked Tulgord Vise.

"Exactly!" chimed Brash Phluster, who, though an artist of modest talents, was not a fool.

"I shall assume the added burden," said I, "in humble acknowledgment of my small role in poor Calap Roud's fate—"

"Small?" snorted Steck Marynd.

"Indeed," I replied, "for did I not state with sure and unambiguous clarity that my tale bears only superficial similarity to our present reality?"

As they all pondered this, Mister Must descended from the carriage, to get his butchering tools from the trunk. A man of many skills, was Mister Must, and almost as practical as Sardic Thew.

Butchering a human was, in detail, little different from butchering any other large animal. The guts must be removed, and quickly. The carcass must be skinned and boned and then bled as best as one is able under the circumstances. This generally involved hanging the quartered sections from the prong hooks at the back end of the carriage, and while this resulted in a spattered trail of blood upon the conveyance's path, why, the symbolic significance was very nearly perfect. In any case, Mister Must worked with proficient alacrity, slicing through cartilage and tendon and gristle, and in no time at all the various pieces that had once been Calap Roud depended dripping from the carriage stern. His head was sent rolling in the direction of the shallow pit containing his hide, organs and intestines.

Does this shock? Look upon the crowd that is your company. Pox the mind with visions of dressed and quartered renditions, all animation drained away. The horror to come in the wake of such imaginings (well, one hopes horror comes) is a complicated mélange. A face of life, a host of words, an ocean of swirling thoughts to brighten active eyes. Grace and motion and a sense that before you is a creature of time (just as you no doubt are), with past, present and future. A single step could set you in his or her sandals, as easy as that. To then jolt one's senses into a realm of butchered meat and red bone, a future torn away, and eyes made dull and empty, ah, is any journey as cruel and disquieting as that one?

To answer: yes, when complimented with the growling of one's own stomach and savory hints wetting the tongue.

Is it cowardice to turn away, to leave Mister Must to his work whilst one admires the sky and horizon, or perhaps frown in vaunted interest at the watchful regard of the horses or the gimlet study from the mules? Certainly not to meet the gaze of anyone else. Cowardice? Absolutely.

Poor Calap Roud. What grief and remorse assails me!

Brash Phluster sidled close as the trek resumed. "That was vicious, Flicker."

"When the mouse is cornered—"

"'Mouse?' Not you. More like a serpent in our midst."

"I am pleased you heeded the warning."

"I bet you are. I could have blurted it out, you know. And you'd have been lying there beside Roud, and I'd be safe."

"Do you wish me to resume my tale, Brash? Recounting all the other lovers of the woman with the brothers?"

"Won't work a second time."

"You would stake your life on Tiny Chanter's self-control?"

Brash licked his lips. "Anyway, now you have two stories, and Purse isn't happy about it. She's disgusted by what you did to Calap. Using her story like that. She feels guilty, too."

"Why, Brash, that is most perceptive."

"She won't be forgiving, not anymore."

"Indeed not."

"I think you're a dead man."

"Brash!" bellowed Tulgord Vise. "Cheer us up! Sing, lad, sing!"

"But we got our supper!"

Tiny Chanter laughed and then said, "Maybe we want dessert. Midge?"

"Dessert."

"Flea?"

"No thanks."

His brothers halted and stared at him. Flea's expression was pained. "I been bunged up now six whole days. I got bits of four people in me, and poets at that. Bad poets."

Tiny's hands twitched. "A dessert will do you good, Flea."

"Honey-glazed," suggested Midge, "if I can find a hive."

Flea frowned. "Maybe an eyeball or two," he conceded.

"Brash!" Tiny roared.

"I got one! Listen, this one's brilliant. It's called 'Night of the Assassin'—"

"Knights can't be assassins," objected Arpo Relent. "It's a rule.

Knights can't be assassins, wizards can't be weapon-masters and mendics got to use clubs and maces. Everyone knows that."

Tulgord Vise frowned. "Clubs? What?"

"No, 'night' as in the sun going down."

"They ride into the sunset, yes, but only at the end."

Brash looked round, somewhat wildly.

"Let's hear it," commanded Tiny.

"Mummumummymummy! Ooloolooloo!"

"Oh sorrow!" came a gargled croak from Sellup, who stumbled along behind the carriage and was now ghostly with dust.

"I was just warming up my singing voice," Brash explained. "Now, 'Night of the Assassin,' by Brash Phluster. An original composition. Lyrics by Brash Phluster, music by Brash Phluster. Composed in the year—"

"Sing or die," said Tiny Chanter.

> *"In the black heart of Malaz City*
> *on a black night of blackness so darrrk*
> *no one could see a thing it was all gritty*
> *when a guard cried out 'harrrrk!'*
>
> *But the darkness did not answer*
> *because no one was therrre*
> *Kalam Mekhar was climbing the tower*
> *instead of using the stairrr*
>
> *The Mad Empress sat on her throne*
> *dreaming up new ways of torturrre*

when she heard a terrible groan
and she did bless the mendic's currre

There was writing carved on the wall
great kings and mad tyrants wrote dire curses
there in the gloomy royal stall
so rank with smeared mercies—"

"She's sitting on a shit-hole?" Tulgord Vise demanded. "Taking a dump?"

"That's the whole point!" Brash retorted. "Everybody sings about kings and princesses and heroes but nobody ever mentions natural bodily functions. I introduced the Mad Empress at a vulnerable moment, you see? To earn her more sympathy and remind listeners she's as human as anybody."

"People know all that," Tulgord said, "and they don't want to hear about it in a damned song about assassins!"

"I'm setting the scene!"

"Let him go on," said Tiny. Then he pointed a culpable finger at Brash. "But no more natural bodily functions."

"Out of the dark night sky
rained down matter most foulll
and Kalam swore and wiped at his eye
wishing he'd brought a towelll

But the chute yawned above him
his way to the Mad Empress was a black hollle

could he but reach the sticky rim
he was but moments from his goallll

In days of yore she was an assassin too
a whore of murder with claws unfurlllled
but now she just needed hard to poo
straining to make her hair currrlll"

"I said—"

"It's part of the story!" squealed Brash Phluster. "I can't help it!"

"Neither could the Empress, seems," added Apto under his breath.

"Kalam looked up then to see a grenado
but swift he was in dodging its plungggge
and he launched up into the brown window
and in the narrow channel he thrashed and lunggged

And climbed and climbed seeking the light
or at least he hoped for some other wayyy
to end the plight of this darkest night
as he prayed for the light of daayyy

Through the narrowest of chutes
he clambered into a pink caverrrnnn
and swam among the furly flukes
'oh,' he cried, 'when will I ever learrnnn?'

Tis said across the entire empire
that the Empress Laseen did give birrthhh
to the Royal Assassins of the Claw entire
you can take that for what it's worrthhh

But Kalam Mekhar knew her better that most
and he did carve his name on her wallll
and we'd all swear he got there first
because we never went there at allll!"

Imagine, if you dare, the nature of the silence that followed "Night of the Assassin." To this very day, all these years later, I struggle and fail to find words of sufficient girth and suitable precision and can only crawl a reach closer, prostrate with nary more than a few gibbering mumbles. We had all halted, I do recall, but the faces on all sides were but a blur, barring that of Sellup, who marched in from a cloud of dust smiling with blackened teeth and said, "Thank you for waiting!"

It is said that as much as the dead will find a way into the ground, so too will they find a way out again. Farmers turn up bones under the plow. Looters shove aside the lid of the crypt and scatter trucked limbs and skulls and such in their hunt for baubles. Sellup, of course, was yet to be buried, but in appearance she was quickly assuming the guise of the interred. Patchy and jellying, her lone brow a snarling fringe above murky matted eyes, various thready remnants of mucous dangling from her crusted nostrils, and already crawling with maggots that had writhed out from her ear-holes to sprinkle her shoulders or choke in the nooses of her tangled hair, she was the kind of fan to elicit a cringe and flinch from the most desperate poet (though sufficiently muted as to avoid too much offense, for we will take what we can get, don't you know).

The curious thing, from the point of view of an artist, lies in the odd reversal a dead fan poses. For the truly adoring worshipper, a favourite artist cursed to an undying existence could well be considered a prayer answered. More songs, more epics, an unending stream of blather and ponce for all eternity! And should the poor poet fall into irreparable decays—a nose falling off, a flap of scalp sagging loose, a certain bloating of intestinal gases followed by a wheezing eruption or two, well, one must suffer for one's art, yes?

We artists who remained, myself and Brash and indeed, even Purse Snippet, we regarded Sellup with an admixture of abhorrence and fascination. Cruel the irony that she adored a poet who was not even around.

No matter. The afternoon stretched on, and of the cloudy thoughts in this collection of cloudy minds, who could even guess? A situation can fast slide into both the absurd and the tragic, and indeed into true horror, and yet for those in its midst, senses adjust in their unceasing search for normality, and so on we go, in our assembly of proper motions, the swing of legs, the thump of heels, lids blinking over dust-stung eyes, and the breath goes in and the breath goes out.

Normal sounds comfort us. Hoofs and carriage wheels, the creak of springs and squeal of axles. Pilgrims upon the trail.

Who, stumbling upon us at that moment, might spare us little more than a single disinterested glance? Walk your own neighbourhood or village street, dear friends, and as you see nothing awry grant yourself a moment and imagine all that you do not see, all that might hide behind the normal moment with its normal details. Do this and you will come to understand the poet's game.

Thoughts to ruminate upon, perhaps, as the twenty-fourth day draws to a close.

A Recounting of the Twenty-fourth Night

"We made good time this day," announced our venerable host, once the evening meal was done and the picked bones flung away into the night. The fire was merry, bellies were full, and out in the dark something voiced curdling cries every now and then, enough to startle Steck Marynd and he would stroke his crossbow like a man with too many barbs on his conscience (What does that mean? Nothing. I just liked the turn of phrase).

"In fact," Sardic Thew continued, beaming above the ruddy flames, "we may well reach the Great Descent to the Landing within a week." He paused, and then added, "Perhaps it is at last safe to announce that our terrible ordeal is over. A few days of hunger, is that too terrible a price to pay for the end to our dread tithe among the living?"

Midge grunted. "What?"

"Well." The host cleared his throat. "The cruel fate of these few remaining poets, I mean."

"What about it?"

Sardic Thew waved his hands. "We can be merciful! Don't you see?"

"What if we don't want to be?" Tiny Chanter asked, grinning greasily (well, in truth he was most fastidious, was Tiny, but given the venal words issuing from those lips, I elected to add the grisly detail. Of course, there is nothing manipulative in this).

"But that—that—that would be—"

"Outright murder?" Apto Canavalian inquired, somewhat too lightly in my opinion.

Brash choked and spat, "It's been that all along, Apto, though when it's not your head on the spitting block, you just go ahead and pretend otherwise."

"I will, thank you."

"Just because you're a judge—"

"Let's get one thing straight," Apto cut in. "Not one of you here is getting my vote. All right? The truth is, there's nothing so deflating as actually getting to know the damned poets I'm supposed to be judging. I feel like a far-sighted fool who finally gets close enough to see the whore in front of him, warts and all. The magic dies, you see. It dies like a dried up worm."

Brash stared with eyes bulging. "You're not going to vote for me?" He leapt to his feet. "Kill him! Kill him next! He's no use to anyone! Kill him!"

As Brash stood trembling, one finger jabbed towards Apto

Canavalian, no one spoke. Abruptly, Brash loosed a sob, wheeling, and ran off into the night.

"He won't go far," opined Steck. "Besides, I happen to agree with our host. The killing isn't necessary any more. It's over—"

"No," said an unexpected voice, "it is not over."

"Lady Snippet," Steck began.

"I was promised," she countered, hands wringing about the cup she held. "He gave me his word."

"So I did," said I. "Tonight, however, I mean to indulge the interests of all here, by concluding poor Calap Roud's tale. Lady, will you abide me until the morrow?"

Her eyes were most narrow in their regard of me. "Perhaps you mean to outlast me. In consideration of that, I will now exact yet another vow from you, Avas Didion Flicker. Before we reach the Great Descent, you will satisfy me."

"So I vow, Milady."

Steck Marynd rose. "I know the tale you will tell tonight," he said to me, and to the others he said, "I will find Nifty Gum and his ladies and bring them back here, for I fear they must be suffering greatly this night."

"Sudden compassion?" said Tulgord Vise with a snort.

"The torment must end," Steck replied. "If I am the only one here capable of possessing guilt, then so be it." And off he went, boots crunching in the gravel.

Guilt. Such an unpleasant word, no doubt invented by some pious meddler with snout pricked to the air. Probably a virgin, too, and not by choice. A man (I assert it must have been a man, since no woman was ever so mad as to invent such a concept, and to this day for most women the whole notion of guilt is as alien to them as flicking droplets after a piss, then shivering), a man, then, likely looking on in outrage and horror (at a woman, I warrant, and given his virginal status she was either his sister or his mother), and bursting into his thoughts like flames from a brimstone, all indignation was transformed into that maelstrom of flagellation, spite, envy, malice and harsh judgement that we have come to call *guilt*. Of course, the accusation, once uttered, is also a declaration of sides. The accuser is a creature of impeccable virtue, a paragon of decency, honour, integrity and intransigence, unsullied and unstained since the moment of birth. Why, flames of purest white blaze from that quivering head, and some force of elevation has indeed lifted the accuser from the ground, feet alight on the air, and somewhere monstrous musicians pound drums of impending retribution. In accusing, the accuser seeks to crush the accused, who in turn has been conditioned to cringe and squirm, to holler and rage, or some frenzied cavort between the two, and misery must result. Abject self-immolation, depression, the wearing of ugliness itself. Whilst the accuser stands, observing, triumphant and quivering in the ecstasy of the righteous. It's as good as sex (but then, what does the virgin know about sex?).

What follows? Why, not much. Usually, nothing. He dozes. She starts chopping dirty carrots or heads out and beats stained garments against a rock (said gestures having no symbolic significance whatsoever). The baby looks on, eating the cat's tail and the cat, knowing nothing of guilt, stares with bemused regard upon the wretched family it has adopted, before realizing that once again the horrid urchin is stuffing it into its mouth, and once again it's time to use the runt as a bed-post. The mind is a dark realm and shadows lurk and creep behind the throne of reason, and none of us sit that throne for long in any case, so let them lurk and creep, what do we care?

"As night came to the Imass camp," said I, "she led the Fenn warrior towards an empty hut which he was free to use as his own until such time that he chose to depart. In the chill darkness she carried a small oil lamp to guide their way, and the flame flickered in the bitter wind, and he strode behind her, his footfalls making no sound. Yet she did not need to turn around to be certain he followed, for she felt the heat of him, like a kiln at her back. He was close, closer than he need be.

"When she ducked through the entrance and then straightened his arms crept round her. She gasped at his touch and arched her back, head against his lowest rib, as his huge hands reached to find her breasts. He was rough in his need, burning with haste, and they descended to the heap of furs unmindful of the cold and damp, the musty smell of the old rushes."

"That nastiness obsesses you!" said Arpo Relent.

"Nastiness, sir?"

"Between a man and a woman, the Unspoken, the Unrevealed, the—"

"Sex, you mean?"

Arpo glared. "Such tales are unseemly. They twist and poison the minds of listeners." He made a fist with one gauntleted hand. "See how Calap Roud died. All it took was a hint of something—"

"I believe I was rather more direct," I said, "although in no way specific, as I had no chance—"

"So you'll do it now! Your mind is a filthy, rotted tumour of lasciviousness! Why, in the city of Quaint your skin would be stripped from your flesh, your weak parts chopped off—"

"Weak parts?"

Arpo gestured between his legs. "That which Whispers Evil Temptation, sir. Chopped off and sealed in a jar. Your tongue would be cut into strips and the Royal Tongs would come out—"

"A little late for those," Apto said, "since you already chopped off the—"

"There is a Worm of Corruption, sir, that resides deep in the body, and if it is not removed before the poor victim dies, it will ride his soul into the Deathly Realm. Of course, the Worm knows when it is being hunted, and it is a master of disguise. The Search often takes days and days—"

"Because the poor man talked about fornication?"

At Apto's query the Well Knight flinched. "I knew you were full of worms, all of you. I'm not surprised. Truly, this is a fallen company."

"Are all poets filled with such corrupting worms?" Apto pressed.

"Of course they are and proof awaits all who succumb to their temptations! The Holy Union resides in a realm beyond words, beyond images, beyond everything!" He gestured in my direction. "These . . . these sullied creatures, they but revel in degraded versions, fallen mockeries. Her hand grasping his *this*, his finger up her *that*. Slavering and dripping and heaving and grunting—these are the bestial escapades of pigs and goats and dogs. And woe to the wretched fool who stirs in the midst of such breathless descriptions, for the Lady of Beneficence shall surely turn her back upon They of Rotten Thoughts—"

"Is it a pretty one?" Apto asked.

Arpo frowned. "Is what pretty?"

"The Lady's back, sir. Curvaceous? Sweetly rounded and inviting—"

With a terrible bellow the Well Knight launched himself at Apto Canavalian. Murder was an onerous mask upon his face, his hair suddenly awry and the gold of his fittings shining with a lurid crimson sheen. Gaunteleted fingers hooked as they lashed out to clutch Apto's rather scrawny neck.

Of course, critics are notoriously difficult to snare, even with their own words. They slip and sidle, prance and dither. So elusive are they that one suspects that they are in fact incorporeal, fey conjurations gathered up like accretions of lint and twigs, ready to burst apart at the first hint of danger. But who, pray tell, would be mad enough to create such snarky homunculi? Why, none other than artists themselves, for in the manner of grubby savages in the deep woods, we slap together our gods from whatever is at hand (mostly fluff) only to eagerly grovel at its misshapen feet (or hoofs), slavering our adoration to hide our true thoughts, which are generally venal.

Sailing over the fire, then, uttering animal roars, Arpo Relent found himself clutching thin air. His hands were still grasping and flaying when his face made contact with the boulder Apto had been leaning against. With noises that would make a potter cringe at the kiln, the Well Knight's steely visage crumpled like sheet tin. Blood sprayed out to form a delicate crescent upon the sun-bleached stone, a glittering halo until his head slid away.

Apto Canavalian had vanished into the darkness.

We who remained sat unmoving. Arpo Relent's fine boots were nicely settled in the fire, suggesting to us that he was unconscious, dead or careless. When the man's leggings caught flame our venerable host leapt forward to drag the limbs clear, grunting as he did so, and then hastily snuffed out the smouldering cloth.

Tiny Chanter snorted and Flea and Midge did the same. From somewhere in the darkness Sellup giggled, and then coughed something up.

Sighing, Tulgord Vise rose, stepped over and crouched beside the Unwell Knight. After a moment's examination, he said, "Alive but senseless."

"Essentially unchanged, then," said Apto, reappearing from the night's inky well. "Made a mess of my rock, though."

"Jest now," Tulgord said. "When he comes to, you're a dead man."

"Who says he'll come to at all?" the critic retorted. "Look how flat his forehead is."

"It was that way before he hit the rock," the Mortal Sword replied.

"Was it leaking snot, too? I think we'd have noticed. He's in a coma and will probably die sometime in the night."

"Pray hard it's so," Tulgord said, looking up with bared teeth.

Apto shrugged, but sweaty beads danced on his upper lip like happy bottle flies.

"You, Flicker," said Tiny Chanter, "you was telling that story. Was finally starting to get interesting."

"Sore stretched indeed," said I, "and maiden no longer—"

"Hold on," Tiny objected, all the flickering flames of the hearth mirrored in his ursine mien. "You can't just skip past all that, unless you don't want to survive the night. Disappointment's a fatal complaint as far as I'm concerned. Disappoint me and I swear I'll kill you, poet."

"I'll kill you, too," said Midge.

"And me," said Flea.

"What pathetic things you Chanters are," said Purse Snippet. Shocked visages numbering three.

Starting and blinking, Relish squinted at her siblings. "What? Someone say something?"

"I called your brothers pathetic," explained the Lady.

"Oh." Relish subsided once more.

Tiny jabbed a blunt finger at Purse Snippet. "You. Watch it."

"Yeah," said Flea. "Watch it."

"You," said Midge. "Yeah."

"The most enticing lure to the imagination," said Purse, "is that which suggests without revealing. This is the true art of the dance, after all. When I perform, I seduce, but that doesn't mean I want to ruffle your sack, unless it's the kind that jingles."

"Making you a tease!" Tulgord growled. "And worse. Tell me, woman, how many murders have you left in your wake? How many broken hearts? Men surrendering to drink after years of abstinence. Imagined rivals knifing each other. How many loving families have you sundered with all that you promise only to then deny? We should never have excluded you from anything—you're the worst of the lot."

Purse Snippet had paled at the Mortal Sword's words.

I did speak then, as proper comportment demanded. "A coward's ambush—shame on you, sir."

The knight stiffened. "Tread softly now, poet. Explain yourself, if you please."

"The tragedies whereof you speak cannot be laid at this lady's delicate feet. They are one and all failures of the men involved, for each has crossed the fatal line between audience and performer. Art is not exclusive in its delivery, but its magic lies in creating the illusion that it has done just that. Speaking only to you. That is art's gift, do you understand, Knight? As such it is to be revered, not sullied. The instant the observer, in appalling self-delusion, seeks to claim for himself that which in truth belongs to everyone, he has committed the greatest crime, one of selfish arrogance, one of unrighteous possession. Before Lady Snippet's performance, this man makes the foulest presumption. Well now, how dare he? Against such a crime it falls to the rest of her adoring audience to place themselves between that man and Lady Snippet."

"As you are doing right now," observed Apto Canavalian (wise in his ways this honourable, highly intelligent and oh-so-observant critic).

Modest the tilt of my head.

Visibly flustered, Tulgord Vise grunted and looked away, chewing at his beard and biting his lip, shifting in discomfort and shuffling his feet and then suddenly finding a kink in the chain of his left vambrace which he set to, humming softly to himself, all of which led me to conclude, with great acuity, that his flusterment was indeed visible.

"I still want details," said Tiny Chanter, glaring at me in canid challenge.

"As a sweet maiden, she was of course unversed in the stanzas of amorous endeavour—"

"What?" asked Midge.

"She didn't know anything about sex," I re-phrased.

"Why do you do that anyway?" Apto inquired.

I took a moment to observe the miserable, vulpine excuse for humanity, and then said, "Do what?"

"Complicate things."

"Perhaps because I am a complicated sort of man."

"But if it makes people frown or blink or otherwise stumble in confusion, what's the point?"

"Dear me," said I, "here you are, elected as Judge, yet you seem entirely unaware of the magical properties of language. Simplicity, I do assert, is woefully overestimated in value. Of course there are times when bluntness suits, but the value of these instances is found in the surprise they deliver, and such surprise cannot occur if they are surrounded in similitude—"

"For Hood's sake," rumbled Tiny, "get back to the other similitudes. The maiden knew nothing so it fell to the Fenn warrior to teach her, and that's what I want to hear about. The world in its proper course through the heavens and whatnot." And he shot Apto a wordless but entirely unambiguous look of warning, that in its mute bluntness succeeded in reaching the critic's murky awareness, sufficient to spark self-preservation. In other words, the look scared him witless.

I resumed. "We shall backtrack, then, to the moment when they stood, now facing one another. He was well-versed—"

"Now it's back to the verses again," whined Midge.

"And though heated with desire," I continued, "he displayed consummate skill—"

"Consummate, yeah!" and Tiny grinned his tiny grin.

From the gloom close to the wagon came Mister Must's gravel-laden voice, "And that's a significant detail, I'll warrant."

So did I twist round then to observe his ghostly visage in its ghostly cloud of rustleaf smoke, catching the knowing twinkle that might have been an eye or a tooth. *Ah, thinks me, a sharp one here. Be careful now, Flicker.*

"Peeling away her clothing, unmindful of the damp chilly air in the guest hut, he laid her bare, his rough fingertips so lightly brushing the pricked awakening of her skin so that she shivered again and again. Her breaths were a rush of quick waves upon a rasping beach, the tremulous water sobbing back as she gasped to his touch where it traveled in eddying swirl about her nipples.

"Her head tilted back, all will abandoned to his sure embrace, the deep and steady breaths that made his chest swell and ease against her. Then his hands edged downward, tracking the lines of her hips, to cup her downy-soft behind, and effortlessly he lifted her—"

"Ha!" barked Tiny Chanter. "Now comes the Golden Ram! The Knob-Headed Dhenrabi rising from the Deep! The Mushroom in the Mulch!"

Everyone stared for a moment at Tiny with his flushed face

and puny but bright eyes. Even Midge and Flea. He looked about, meeting stare after stare, a little wildly, before scowling and gesturing to me. "Go on, Flicker."

"She cried out as if ripped asunder, and blood started, announcing the death of her childhood, but he held her in his strong hands to keep her safe from true injury—"

"How tall was she again?" Flea asked.

"About knee-high," Apto answered.

"Oh. Makes sense then."

Relish laughed, ill-timed indeed as her brothers suddenly glared at her.

"You shouldn't be listening to this," Tiny said. "Losing maidenhood ain't like that. It's all agony and aches and filth and slow oozing of deadly saps, and shouldn't be undertaken without supervision—"

"What, you think you're gonna *watch*?" Relish demanded, flaring up like the seed-head of a thistle in a brush fire. "If I'd known brothers were like this, I would have killed you all long ago!"

"It's our responsibility!" snarled Tiny, that finger back up and jabbing. "We promised Da—"

"Da!" Relish shrieked. "Till his dying day he never figured out the connection between babies and what he and Ma did twice a year!" She waved heir arms like a child sitting on a bee hive. "Look at us! Even I don't know how many brothers I got! You were dropping like apples! Everywhere!"

"Watch what you're saying about Da!"

"Yeah, watch it!"

"Yeah! Da!"

Relish suddenly crossed her arms and smirked. "Responsible, that's a joke. If you knew anything, well, ha ha. Ha!"

I cleared my throat most delicately. "He left her exhausted, curled up in his arms, stung senseless with love. And much of the night passed unwitnessed for our lovely woman for whom innocence was already a fading memory."

"That is the way of it," Tulgord Vise said with solemn nod. "When they lose that innocence to some grinning bastard from the next village, suddenly they can't get enough of it, can they? That . . . that other stuff. Rutting everything in sight, that's what happens, and that boy who loved her since they were mere whelplings, why, all he can do is look on, knowing he'll never get to touch her ever again, because there's a fierce fire in her eyes now, and a swagger to her walk, a looseness to her hips, and she's not interested anymore in playing hide and seek down by the river, and if she turned up all slack-faced and drowned down on the bank, well, whose fault was that? After all, she wasn't innocent no more, was she? No, she was the opposite of that, yes, assuredly she was. The Sisters smile at whores, did you know that? They are soft that way. Innocent, no, she wasn't that. The opposite." He looked up. "And what's the opposite of innocence?"

And into the grim silence, in voice cool and low did I venture: "Guilt?"

Some tales die with a wheezy sigh. Some are stabbed through the heart. At least for a time. It was late and for some, dreadfully too late. In solitude and in times broken and husked and well rooted in contemplation, we find the necessity to regard our deeds, and see for ourselves all that which ever abides, this garden of scents both sweet and vaguely rotting. Some lives die with a sated sigh. Some are drowned in a river.

Others get eaten by the righteous.

At certain passages in the night the darkness grows vapid, a desultory, pensive state that laps energy like a bat's flicking tongue a cow's pricked ankle. Somnolent the wandering steps, brooding the regard, drowsy this disinterest. Until in the murk one discerns a tapestry scene of the like to adorn a torturer's bedroom.

A mostly naked woman stood in fullest profile, her arms raised overhead, balanced in her hands a rather large boulder, whilst directly below, at her very feet, was proffered the motionless head of a sleeping sibling.

Soft as my approach happened to be, Relish heard and glanced over. "Just like this," she whispered. "And . . . done."

"You have held this pose before, I think."

"I have. Until my arms trembled."

"I imagine," I ventured, drawing closer, "you have contemplated simply running away."

She snorted, twisted to one side and sent the boulder thumping and bounding through some brushes in the dark. "You don't know them. They'd hunt me down. Even if there was only one of them left, I'd be hunted down. Across the world. Under the seas. To the hoary moon itself." She fixed wounded, helpless eyes upon me. "I am a prisoner, with no hope of escape. Ever."

"I understand that it does seem that way right now—"

"Don't give me that steaming pile of crap, Flicker. I've had my fill of brotherly advice."

"Advice was not my intention, Relish."

Jaded her brow. "You hungry for another roll? We damned near killed each other last time."

"I know and I dream of it still and will likely do so until my dying day."

"Liar."

I let the accusation rest, for to explain that the dream wasn't necessarily a pleasant one, would have, in my esteem, been untimely. I'm sure you agree.

"So, not advice."

"A promise, Relish. To free you of their chains before this journey ends."

"Gods below, is this some infection or something? You and promises to women. The secret flaw you imagine yourself so clever at hiding—"

"I hide nothing—"

"So bold and steady-eyed then, thus making it the best of disguises." She shook her head. "Besides, such afflictions belong to pimply boys with cracking voices. You're old enough to know better."

"I am?"

"Never promise to save a woman, Flicker."

"Oh, and why?"

"Because when you fail, she will curse your name for all time, and when you happen to succeed, she'll resent you for just as long. A fool is a man who believes love comes of being owed."

"And this afflicts only men?"

"Of course not. But I was talking of you."

"The fool in question."

"That's where my theories fall apart—the ones about you, Flicker. You're up to something here."

"Beyond plain survival?"

"No one's going to kill you on this journey. You have made sure of that."

"I have?"

"You snared me and Brash using the old creep, Calap Roud. You hooked Purse Snippet. Now you shamed Tulgord Vise and he needs you alive to prove to you you're wrong about him." She looked down at Tiny. "And even him, he's snagged, too, because he's not as stupid as he sounds. Just like Steck, he's riding on your words, believing there are secrets in them. Your magic— that's what you called it, isn't it?"

"I can't imagine what secrets I possess that would be of any use to them."

She snorted again. "If anybody wants to see you dead and mute, it's probably Mister Must."

Well now, that was a cogent observation indeed. "Do you wish to be freed of your brothers or not?"

"Very deft, Flicker. Oh, why not? Free me, sweet hero, and you'll have my gratitude and resentment both, for all time."

"Relish, what you do with your freedom is entirely up to you, and the same for how you happen to think about the manner in which it was delivered. As for me, I will be content to witness, as might a kindly uncle—"

"Did you uncle me the other night, Flicker?"

"Dear me, I should say not, Relish." And my regard descended to Tiny's round face, so childlike in brainless repose. "You are certain he sleeps?"

"If he wasn't, your neck would already be snapped."

"I imagine you are correct. Even so. It is late, Relish, and we have far to walk come the morrow."

"Yes, Uncle."

Watching her walk off to find her bedding, I contemplated myriad facets of humanly nature, as I selected the opposite direction in which to resume my wandering. Capemoths circled over my head like the bearers of grim thoughts, which I shooed away with careless gestures. The moon showed its smudged face to the east, like a wink through mud. Somewhere off to my right, lost in the gloom, Sellup was singing to herself as she stalked the night, as the undead will do.

Is there anything more fraught than family? We do not choose our kin, after all, and even by marriage one finds oneself saddled with a whole gaggle of new relations, all gathered to witness the fresh mixing of blood and, if of proper spirit, get appallingly drunk, sufficient to ruin the entire proceedings and to be known thereafter in infamy. For myself, I have always considered this gesture, offered to countless relations on their big day, to be nothing more than protracted revenge, and have of course personally partaken of it many times. Closer to home, as it were, why, every new wife simply adds to the wild, unwieldy clan. The excitement never ends!

Even so, poor Relish. Flaw or not, I vowed that I would have to do something about it, and if this be my weakness, then so be it.

"Flicker!"

The hiss brought me to a startled halt. "Brash?"

The gangly poet emerged from night's felt, his hair upright and stark, thorn-scratches tracked across his drawn cheeks, his tongue darting to wet his lips and his ears twitching at imagined sounds. "Why didn't anyone kill him?"

"Who?"

"Apto Canavalian! Who won't vote for any of us. The worst kind of judge there is! He wastes the ground he stands upon!"

"Arpo Relent attempted the very thing you sought, dear poet, and, alas, failed—perhaps fatally."

Brash Phluster's eyes widened. "The Well Knight's dead?"

"His Wellness hangs in the balance."

"Just what he deserves!" snarled the poet. "That murderous bag of foul wind. Listen! We could just run—this very night. What's to stop us? Steck's lost somewhere—who knows, maybe Nifty and his fans jumped him. Maybe they all killed each other out there in the desert."

"You forget, good sir, the Chanters and, of course, Tulgord Vise. I am afraid, Brash, that we have no choice but to continue on—"

"If Arpo dies, we can eat him, can't we?"

"I don't see why not."

"And maybe that'll be enough. For everyone. What do you think?"

"It's certainly possible. Now, Brash, take yourself to bed."

He raked his fingers through his hair. "Gods, it's not fair how us artists are treated, is it? They're all vultures! Don't they see how every word is a tortured excretion? Our sweat drips red, our blood pools and blackens beneath our finger nails, our teeth loosen at night and we stagger through our dreams gumming our words. I write and lose entire manuscripts between dusk and dawn—does that happen to you? Does it?"

"That it does, friend. We are all cursed with ineffable genius. But consider this, perhaps we each are in fact not one, but many, and whilst we sleep in this realm another version of us wakens to another world's dawn, and sets quill to parchment—the genius forever beyond our reach is in fact his own talent, though he knows it not and like you and I, he frets over the lost works of his nightly dreams."

Brash was staring at me with incredulous eyes. "That is cruelty without measure, Flicker. How could you even imagine such diabolical things? A thousand other selves, all equally tortured and tormented! Gods below!"

"I certainly do not see it that way," did I reply. "Indeed, the notion leads me to ever greater efforts, for I seek to join all of our voices into one—perhaps, I muse, this is the truth of real, genuine genius. My myriad selves singing in chorus, oh how I long to be deafened by my own voice!"

"Yearn away," Brash said, with a sudden wicked grin. "You're doomed, Flicker. You just made me realize something, you see. I am already deafened by my own voice, meaning I already am a genius. Your argument proves it!"

"Thank goodness for that. Now, sing yourself off to sleep, Brash Phluster, and we will speak more of this upon the morning."

"Flicker, do you have a knife?"

"Excuse me?"

"I'm going to make Apto vote for me even if I have to kill him to do it."

"That would be murder, friend."

"We are awash in blood already, you fool! What's one little dead critic more? Who'd miss him? Not me. Not you."

"A dead man cannot vote, Brash."

"I'll force him to write a proxy note first. Then we can eat him."

"I sincerely doubt he would prove palatable. No, Brash Phluster, you will receive no weapon from me."

"I hate you."

Off he stormed, in the manner of a golit bird hunting snakes.

"His mind has cracked." With this observation, Purse Snippet appeared, her cloak drawn tight about her lithe form.

"Will no one sleep this night?" I asked, in some exasperation.

"Our cruel and unhappy family is in tatters."

To this I grunted.

"Do doubts finally afflict you, Avas Didion Flicker? I intend no mercy, be certain of that."

"The burdens are weighty indeed, Lady Snippet, but I remain confident that I shall prevail."

She drew still closer, her eyes searching mine, as women's eyes are in the habit of doing when close we happen to stand. What secret promise are they hoping to discover? What fey hoard of untold riches do they yearn to pry open? Could they but imagine the murky male realm lurking behind these lucid pearls, they might well shatter the night with shrieks and flee into the shelter of darkness itself. But this is the mystery of things, is it not? We bounce through guesses and hazy uncertainties, and call it rapport, bridged and stitched with smiles and engaging expressions, whilst behind both set of eyes maelstroms rage benighted in wild images of rampant sex and unlikely trysts. Or so I fancy, and why not? Such musings are easy vanquish over probable truths (that at least one of us is either bored rigid or completely mindless with all the perspicacity of a jellyfish, and oft I have caught myself in rubbery wobble, mind, or even worse: is that intensity merely prelude to picking crabs from my eyebrows? Oh yes, we stand close and behind our facades we quiver in trepid tremulosity, even as our mouths flap a league a breath).

Where were we? Ah yes, standing close, her eyes tracking mine like twin bows with arrows fixed, whilst I shivered like two hares in lantern light.

"How, then," asked Purse Snippet (eyes tracking . . . tracking—I am pinned!), "do you intend to save me, noble sir? In the manner of all those others, in a tangle of warm flesh and the oblivion of sated desires? Have you any idea just how many men I have had? Not to mention women? And each time a new candidate steps forth, what do I see in those oh-so-eager eyes?" She slowly shook her head. "The conviction writ plain that this one can do what none before was capable of doing, and what must I then witness?"

"I would hazard, the pathetic collapse of such brazen arrogance?"

"Yes. But here, and now, I look into your eyes and what do I see?"

"To be honest, Lady, I have no idea."

"Really."

"Really."

"I don't believe you."

Do you see? She had crowbar in hand, the treasure chest looms (mine, not hers, we're being figurative here. We'll get to the literal in a moment), and the lock looks flimsy indeed. And in her eyes what do I see? Why, the conviction that she and she alone has what it takes (whatever it takes, don't ask me), to crack loose that mysterious lockbox of fabulous revelations that is, well, the real me.

Bless her.

Do you all finally understand my angst? I mean, is this all there is? What is *this* anyway? I don't know. Ask my wives. They pried me loose long ago, to their eternal disappointment, of which they continually remind me, lest I stupidly wander into some impractical daydream (such as this: Is there some woman out there who still thinks me mysterious? I must find her! That kind of daydream). As tired old philosophers say, the scent is ever sweeter over the garden wall. And my, how we do climb.

What a tirade of cynicism! I am not like this at all, I do assure you. I have this lockbox hidden inside me, you see . . . do come find it, will you?

It is a sage truth that there can never be too many disappointed wives.

Her lips found mine. Have I missed something? I have not.

Quick as a cat upon a mouse, a cock upon a snail, a crow upon a sliver of dead meat. And her tongue went looking for the treasure chest. She didn't believe me, recall? They never do.

In my weakness, which I call upon in times of need, I could not resist.

Was she the most beautiful woman I ever knowingly shared fluids with? She was indeed. Shall I recount the details? I shall not. In protection of her sweet modesty, of that luscious night my lips shall remain forever sealed.

Oh, forget that. I cupped her full breasts, which is what men do for some unknown reason, except perhaps that it has something to do with the way we gauge value, upon scales as it were, replete with aesthetic appreciation, engineering terminology and so on. With a dancer's grace (and muscle) she drew one meaty thigh up along my left hip, grinding her mound against my crotch with an undulating, circular gyration that snapped the buttons of my collar and burst seams everywhere. With nefarious insistence, that leg somehow wrapped itself to rest athwart my buttocks (*buttocks*, what a maddeningly absurd word), her taut calf appearing upon my right, curling round (was this even possible?) to hook over my hip. If this was not outrageous enough, the very foot at the end of that selfsame leg suddenly plunged beneath my breeches to snare the rearing tubeworm of my weakness, between big toe and the rest.

At this point, she'd already closed one hand about the bag and was rolling the marbles to and fro, whilst her other hand was driving a finger against previously unexplored areas of sexual sensitivity in that dubious crack people of all genders cannot help but possess.

And my thoughts at this stage in the proceedings? Picture, if you will, a newborn's expression of interminable stunned witless stupidity, wide as a bright smile following wind, eyes spread to the wonder of it all when every bit of that "all" is entirely beyond comprehension. If you have reared children or suffered the fate of caring for someone else's, then you know well the look I faint describe herein. This was the state of my organ of thought. Immune to all intrusion as my clothing miraculously melted away and she mounted herself smooth as perfumed silk, only to suddenly pull free, unwind herself with serpent grace, and step back.

"You get the rest when I am redeemed."

Women.

I am at a loss for words. Even all these decades later. At a loss. Forgive.

For all our conceits we are, in the end, helpless creatures. We grasp all that is within reach, and then yearn for all beyond that reach. In said state, how can we hope for redemption? Staggering off to my bedroll, I slept fitfully that night, and was started awake just before dawn when Steck Marynd returned on his weary horse, the trundled form of Nifty Gum straddling the beast's rump.

Mild and fleeting my curiosity at the absence of the Entourage, until exhaustion plucked me free of the miserable world one last time before the sun rose to announce the twenty-fifth day upon Cracked Pot Trail.

A Recounting of the Twenty-fifth Day

His face bleak, Steck Marynd crouched before the ash-heaped hearth, and told his tale whilst we gnawed on what was left of Calap Roud. Bludgeoning the heat with the sun barely squatting on the eastern hills. Turgid the dusted air through which crazed insects flitted. Squalid and pinched these faces on pilgrimage to expressions of ecstatic release. Unmindful the implacable mules and unhampered the innocent horses.

The host sat in fret. Tiny, Midge and Flea crouched and picked like rock-apes over the last of the unspoiled meat. Relish braided blades of grass, making small nooses. Mister Must puttered about the carriage, pausing to scratch his backside every now and then, before adding more leaves to the pot of tea, stirring and whatnot. Apto Canavalian huddled beneath his threadbare blanket, as if withering beneath the murderous glares of Brash Phluster. Purse Snippet sipped at her steaming cup and a hand and a foot was visible from the ditch where Sellup was lying.

Tulgord Vise paced, fondling his pommel as knights will do.

Arpo Relent, alas, had not moved a single twitch from his facedown deliberations, and this was ominous indeed.

As for Nifty Gum, why, from what could be seen in that bunch and fold of cloak, that haystack of once glistening gold hair now as disheveled as a hairball spat up by a dragon, he was at the very edge of gibbering unreason, as might afflict a famous person no-one wanted to know anymore. Buffeted by our disregard, he sat like an overgrown milestone, head lowered, hands hidden, his boots splashed with dark stains and churning with flies.

Steck Marynd prefaced his recount with a shudder and hands up at his face, as if in horror of memories resurrected. Then he lowered those weathered hands, revealing a visage of guttered faith, and began.

I am a man of doubts, though with eyes set upon me none would say such a thing. Is this not fair? Stalwart and firm, is Steck Marynd. Slayer of demons, hunter of necromancers, the very spine of the Nehemothanai—you will be silent, Mortal Sword, for even you must accept that this is a bloodied trail I have followed far longer than you. I am the cutter excising the cancer of evil, the surgeon setting blade to the tumour of cold malice. Such is the course of my life. I have chosen it and do not begrudge this nest of scars.

Yet, there are doubts within me, the begat of the very life I have chosen for myself. I tell you all this: when one looks into the eye of evil, one's very soul is shaken, and trembles but one tug from uprooted and forever lost. The ground becomes uncertain underfoot. Balance tilts awry. To then strike it down, to destroy it utterly, is an act of self-preservation. In defense of one's own soul. It is like that. Each and every time. But there are moments when it is not enough, not nearly enough.

Are we the children of gods? If so, then what god would so countenance such ignoble spawn? Why is the proper and good path so narrow, so disused, while the cruel and wanton ones proliferate in endless swarm? Why is the choice of integrity the thinnest branch within reach? While the dark wild tree is a mad web across half the sky?

Oh, yes, I know. You poets will sing to me of value gauged in the strain of the challenge, as if sheer difficulty is the meaning of worth. If righteousness was easy, you say, it would not shine like gold. And do not beggars dream of gold, just as the fallen dream of salvation, and the coward dreams of courage? But you do not understand anything. Do the gods exult in the temptations they fling before us? Why? Are they insane? Are they, in fact, eager to see us fall? Give us the clear and true path, and in the act of seeing the darkness falls away, the lures vanish, the way home beckons us all.

If you would awaken our souls, dear gods, be so good as to then sweep the shadows from the road ahead.

No, the gods have all the moral rectitude of children. They created nothing and are no different from us, knuckled to the world.

Listen! I have no faith in any of you. And naught in me either. Do none of you see how this pilgrimage has already failed? Oh, easy enough for the poets to comprehend that hoary truth—seeking fame we step into their path and cut them down, and then gnaw on their bones. And what of you, Sardic Thew? And you, Lady Snippet? And the Dantoc and her footman? You have eaten of the flesh and it was the easiest road of all, wasn't it? And who stood tallest with armoured excuses? Why, none other than Tulgord Vise, Champion of Purity, and indeed the Well Knight Arpo Relent, paladin of virtue.

One day I shall stand before the Nehemoth, before Bauchelain and Korbal Broach. I shall look upon true evil. And they will see in my eyes all the evil that I have done, and they will smile and call me friend. Companion. Cohort in the League of Venality. Could I deny them?

Faith? Look upon Nifty Gum, this broken thing here. An artist beloved, so beloved his retinue of worshippers would bare fangs against the envy of the gods themselves.

I found their trail, even as the shadows of dusk closed in. A rampant, rabid thing, skittering this way and that, a small herd led by a blind bull. Rocks overturned, plants torn loose—yes, they hungered. They thirsted. And suffered. Two women, the man they honoured with their loyalty.

In darkness I came upon their first camp, and from the scuffs and signs I was able to reconstruct the dreadful events with nary a test to my woodsmanship. See me claw my face yet again?

The youngest was set upon, the other two in cahoots, a pact forged in a demon's hole, that one. The innocent child, strangled, all the soft parts of her sweet form torn away by savage teeth. *Teeth.* Ah, Midge, do I see you pause in your breaking fast? Well you should. You see, when those eager mouths drank and fed, poor Oggle Gush was not yet dead.

They ate themselves sick, did Pampera and Nifty. And they left the body in their wake, spoiled, rotting. I see your shock, Brash Phluster, and I do mock it. If you had but one adoring fan in your wake, and starvation loomed, you would not hesitate— deny it not! See Nifty Gum, huddled there. No hesitation stuttered his hands.

When I renewed my tracking, I admit my thoughts were black as a pauper's pit. Now, I did hunt. I believed I could forge this distinction, you see, between what they had done to that child, and all that we have done on this here trail. Is not the soul a thing of sweet conceit?

So now, consider this. He had but one worshipper left, and she was close in that she shared his crime, a murderess, a belly-bloated beauty he could touch with familiarity so absolute no mortal could step between them. You might think. And you might fold tight your arms and whisper easing words to yourself. She but followed his lead—what else could she do, after all?

Was it guilt, then, that launched her upon his back? That sank teeth into his shoulder, striving towards his throat? The mouthfuls of spurting flesh she gobbled down, even as he shrieked and thrashed? And what of Nifty Gum? That he should twist round and bite her in turn, fatally as it transpired, snipping through her jugular, whereupon he bathed and did drink deep. Even as she died, she gnawed upon his right calf, and so was left in a pose of blessed defiance.

I caught him twenty paces down from this final atrocity, limping and streaming crimson. Oh yes, all of you set eyes upon him now. This poet of appetites. Study him in your arrayed expressions of horror and disgust. Hypocrites one and all. You. Me. The wretched gods, too. Aye, I should have killed him then and there. A quarrel through the back of his head. I should have. But no. Why should the blood stain my hands alone? I give him to you, pilgrims. He is the end of this path, the one we have all chosen. I give him to you all. My gift.

As his last words drifted and sank into earth and flesh, Brash Phluster licked his lips and said, "But, where is she? Can't we still—"

"No," growled Mister Must, in a tone that stirred awake his soldier days, "we cannot, Phluster."

"But I don't want to die!"

And at that, Steck Marynd did weep.

For myself, I admit to a certain satisfaction. Oh, don't look at me like that! Given the chance, what artist wouldn't eat his fans? Think of the satisfaction! Far preferable than the opposite, I fervently assert. But let us skip and dance from such admissions, lest they unveil things even more unsightly.

Sellup crawled from the ditch, her split lips stretched back in a ghastly smile, her eyes fixing upon Nifty Gum. "All for me!" she cackled, dragging herself closer. "I won't eat you, darling! I'm not even hungry!"

The wretched poet, thrice named Artist of the Century, lifted his bedraggled head. The modest balance of his features was gone, each detail inexpertly reassembled into a pastiche of Gumdom. Old blood stained his chin, flaked the edges of his tunneled mouth. Flanking the ill-ruddered nose, each eye struggled with the other, fighting over proper alignment, which neither could quite manage. And if a lockbox waited behind those orbs, it was kicked over, contents strewn in tangled heaps. From the weep of his crusted nostrils to the coagulated clumps in his stringy hair, he was indeed a man bereft of his Entourage, barring one dead hag avowing undying servitude.

"It was the eggs," he whispered.

At this even Sellup paused.

"I was so hungry. All I could think of was . . . was *eggs!* Sunny side up, scrambled, poached." Trembling fingertips touched his mouth and he flinched, as if those fingers did not belong to him at all. "Those tales. A dragon spawn trapped in a giant egg— that's just *stupid*. I—I don't even like meat! Not real meat. But eggs, that's different. Like an idea not yet born, I could eat those. I so want to! It was the maiden he stole. The Egg Demon, I mean. Stole—stole away in the night! I tried to warn them, you see, I really did. But they wouldn't listen!" He stabbed a finger at Sellup. "You! You wouldn't listen! I'm out of ideas, don't you see that!? Why do you think I plundered every fairy tale I could find? It's—it's—*all gone!*"

"I'll be your egg, sweetie!" She picked up a rock and rapped it against the side of her head, eliciting a strange muted thump. "Crack me open, darling! See? It's easy!"

As one might imagine, we stared in morbid fascination at this tableau and all its bizarre logic, and I was reminded of that cabal of poets from Aren a few centuries back, the ones who imbibed all manner of hallucinogens in a misplaced search for enlightenment, only to get lost in the private weirdness that is the artist's mortal brain when it can discern nothing but its own navel (and who needs hallucinogens for that?).

"Get away from me."

"Sweetie!" *Thump-thump.* "Here take my rock!" *Thump!* "You can do it too!" *Thump!* "It's easy!"

As it turned out, even Nifty Gum was of no mind to discover what hid inside the skull of one of his fans. Instead, he whispered, "Someone end it. Please. Someone. Plea—"

I would hazard the notion that this heartfelt utterance referred to a wholly natural desire to see Sellup expunged from his (and everyone else's) sight, and in that regard Nifty won my sympathies entire. For reasons unknown, however (oh how I lie, don't I?), Tulgord Vise misinterpreted the Great Artist and in answer he thrust his sword between the poet's shoulder blades. The point burst from Nifty's chest in a welter of blood and splintered bone.

Nifty's eyes gave up the struggle, and he sagged, leaning heavily on the sword blade before, with a grunt, Tulgord heaved the weapon free. The poet fell back in a puff of dust.

Sellup moaned. "Thumbsy?"

Seeing the man's lips moving, I edged closer—after a wary

glance Tulgord's way, but he was already cleaning his blade in the sand beside the trail—and then I leaned close. "Nifty? It is me, Flicker."

Sudden horror lit up Nifty's eyes. "The eggs," he breathed. *"The eggs!"*

Whereupon, with a strange, blissful smile, he died.

Is this the fate for all artists who wantonly steal inspiration? Certainly not, and shame on you for even suggesting it.

Our family was indeed in tatters. But this morning was yet to give up the last of its shocking revelations, for at that moment Well Knight Arpo Relent sat up, blinking the gobs of mucous from his eyes. The crack in his head dripped pink tears, but he seemed unmindful of that.

"Who dressed me?" he demanded in an odd voice.

Apto Canavalian lifted his gaze, and a most forlorn and dejected gaze it was. "Your mother?"

Arpo stood, somewhat unsteadily, and tugged clumsily at the straps of his armour. "I don't need this."

Poor Sellup had resumed her crawling and was now curled up on Nifty's sundered chest, tentatively licking at the blood. "Look at this," she muttered, "I have no taste at all."

"Well Knight," said Tulgord Vise, "do you recall what happened to you?"

At that Apto Canavalian started, and then stared up at the Mortal Sword in horror commingled with blistering hatred.

"The blood dried up," Arpo answered. "Miserable shits, after all I did for them. Open the flood gates! Who pissed on that altar? Was that a demon did that? I hate demons. Death to all demons!" He succeeded in shucking off his coat of mail and it fell to one side with a golden rustle. "All dogs must hereafter walk backwards. That's my decree and make of it what you will. Pluck one eye from every cat, bring them in buckets—of course I'm serious! No, not the cats, the eyes. It's tragic the dogs can't see where they're going. So, we take those eyes and we—"

"Well Knight!"

Arpo glared at Tulgord Vise. "Who in Farl's name are you?"

"Wrong question!" the Mortal Sword snapped. "Who are *you?*"

"Well now, what's this?"

We all stared at what Relent now gripped in one hand.

"That's your penis," said Apto Canavalian. "And I say that advisedly."

Arpo stared down at it. "Kind of explains everything, doesn't it?"

Personally, I see no humour in that statement whatsoever. In any case, Arpo Relent (or whoever happened to be inhabiting his body at that time) now focused his entire attention upon his discovery, and moments later made a mess of things. His brows lifted, and then he smiled and started over again. "I could do this all day. In fact, I think I will."

With a disgusted grunt Tulgord Vise turned to saddle his horse.

Sardic Thew clapped his hands. "Well! I think today's the day!"

Tiny Chanter belched. "Better not be. Flicker's got stories to finish and he ain't getting away with not finishing them."

"Dear sir," said I, "we have the breadth of the sun's passage, if our host's assessment is correct and why would we doubt it? Fear not, resolutions abound."

"If I don't like what I hear you're a dead man."

"Yeah," said Fl—oh, never mind.

Studiously, I avoided Purse Snippet's piercing regard, only to be speared by Relish's. The maddening expectations of women!

As if chilled, Apto Canavalian drew tighter his cloak. He rose to stand close to me. "Flicker, a word if you please."

"You need fear nothing from Brash Phluster, sir." I raised my voice. "Is that not true, Brash?"

The young poet's face twisted. "I just want things to be fair, Flicker. Tell him that. Fair. I deserve that. We both do, you and me. Tell him that."

"Brash, he is standing right here."

"I'm not talking to him."

Apto was gesturing, clearly wanting the two of us to walk off a short distance. I glanced around. Mister Must had reappeared with his tea pot. Sardic Thew held out his cup with shaky hands, whilst Purse Snippet offered the old man a frail smile as he went to her first. Our host's visage flashed dark for a moment. Relish was now braiding a whole string of nooses together, reminding me of the winter solstice ritual of an obscure Ehrlii tribe, something to do with hanging charms upon a tree in symbolic remembrance of when they used to hang bigger things from trees. Her brothers were throwing small rocks at Sellup's head, laughing when one struck. The deathless fan, however, gave no indication of noticing, busy as she was eating Nifty's heart out. Steck Marynd sat staring at the ashes of the campfire, and all the knuckle bones that glowed like infernal coals.

Arpo Relent had worked his penis into exhaustion and was now slapping the limp tip back and forth with all the hopeless optimism of an unsated woman on a wedding night.

"We have a few moments yet, it seems," I conceded. "Lead on, sir."

"I never wanted to be a judge," Apto said once we'd gone about twenty paces up the trail. "I shouldn't be here at all. Do you have any idea how hard it is being a critic?"

"Why, no. Is it?"

The man shivered in the wretched heat, leading me to wonder if he was fevered. "It's what eats at us all, you see."

"No, I am afraid I don't."

His eyes flicked at mine. "If we could do what you do, don't you think we would?"

"Ah."

"It's like the difference between a fumbling adolescent and a master lover. We're brilliant in squirts, while you can enslave a woman across the span of an entire night. The truth is, we hate you. In the unlit crevices of our cracked soul, we seethe with resentment and envy—"

"I would not see it that way, Apto. There are many kinds of talent. A sharp eye and a keen intellect, why, they are rare enough to value in themselves, and their regard set upon us is our reward."

"When you happen to like what we say."

"Indeed. Otherwise, why, you're an idiot and it gives us no small amount of pleasure to say so. As far as relationships go," I added, "there is little that is unique or even at all unusual here."

"All right, it's like this, this here, this very conversation we're having."

"I'm sorry?"

"'Entirely lacking profundity, touching on philosophical issues with the subtlety of a warhammer. Reiterations of the obvious'—see my brow lifting to show just how unimpressed I am? So, what do you think I'm really saying when I make such pronouncements?"

"Well, I suppose you're saying that in fact you are smarter than me—"

"Sharper than your dull efforts to be sure. Wiser, cooler of regard, loftier, far too worldly to observe your clumsy maunderings with anything but amused condescension."

"Surely it is your right to think so."

"Don't you feel a stab of hate, though?"

"Ah, but the wise artist—and indeed, some of us *are* wise—possesses a most perfect riposte, one that pays no regard to whatever murky motives lie behind such attacks."

"Really? What is it?"

"Well, before I answer let me assure you that this in no way refers to you, for whom I feel affection and growing respect. That said, why, we forge a likeness in our tale and then proceed to excoriate and torture the hapless arse-hole with unmitigated and relentless contempt."

"The ego's defense—"

"Perhaps, but I am content enough to call it *spite*."

And Apto, being a critic whom as I said I found both amiable and admirable (shock!), was grinning. "I look forward to the conclusion of your tales this day, Avas Didion Flicker, and you can be assured that I will consider them most carefully as I ponder the adjudication of the Century's Greatest Artist."

"Ah, yes, rewards. Apto Canavalian, do you believe that art possesses relevance in the real world?"

"Now, that is indeed a difficult question. After all, whose art?"

To that I shrugged. "Pray, don't ask me."

All chill had abandoned Apto upon our return to the others. Light his step and fair combed his hair. Brash Phluster bared his teeth upon seeing the transformation, and stewed to a boil of suspicion was his glare in my direction. Mister Must was already perched and waiting atop the carriage, small clouds of smoke rising from his pipe. Steck Marynd sat astride his horse, crossbow resting across one forearm. He wore his soldier's mask once again, angled sharp with a strew of discipline and stern determination. Indeed, backlit by the morning sun, the exudation surrounding this grim figure was an aura of singular purpose, a penumbra ominous as a jilted woman's upon the doorstep of a rival's house.

Tulgord Vise was in turn swinging himself onto his mount in a jangle of chain and deadly weapons. Stalwart in pose, vigorous in defense of propriety, the Mortal Sword of the Sisters cast grating eyes upon the much-reduced party, and allowed himself a satisfied nod.

"Is this my horse?" Arpo Relent asked, glaring at the beast that still stood barebacked and hobbled.

"Gods below," growled Tulgord. "You, Flicker, saddle the thing, else we linger here all day. And you, Phluster, give us a song."

"Nobody has to die anymore!"

"That's what you think," retorted Tiny Chanter. "The Reaver himself is your audience, poet, as it should be. A blade hovers over your head. A sneer announces your death sentence, a yawn spells your doom. A modest drift of attention from any one of us and your empty skull rolls and bounces on the road. Hah, this is how performance *should* be! Life in the balance!"

"And if was you?" snarled Brash in sudden courage (or madness).

"I wouldn't waste my time in poetry, you fool. Words—why, anyone can put them together, in any order they please. It's not like what you're doing is hard, is it? The rest of us just don't bother. We got better things to do with our time."

"I take it," ventured Apto, "as a king you are not much of a patron to the arts."

"Midge?"

"He arrested the lot," said Midge.

"Flea?"

"And then boiled them alive, in a giant iron pot."

"The stink," said Midge.

"For days," said Flea.

"Days," said Midge.

"Now, poet. Sing!" And Tiny smiled.

Brash whimpered, clawed at his greasy mane of hair. "Gotho's Folly, the Lullaby Version, then."

"The what?"

"I'm not talking to you! Now, here it is and no interruptions please.

> *"Lie sweet in your cot, precious onnne*
> *The dead are risin from every graaave*
> *The dead are risin, I say, from every graaa-yev!*
> *Bright your little eyes, precious onnne*
> *Bright as beacons atop that barrowww*
>
> *"Stop your screamin, precious onnne*
> *The dead ain't deaf they can hear you fine*
> *Oh the dead ain't deaf I say, they hear you fiii-yen!*
> *Stop your climbin, precious onnne*
> *Sweet it's gonna taste your oozin marrowww*
>
> *Oh we never wanted you anywayyy—"*

"Enough!" roared Tulgord Vise, wheeling his horse round as he unsheathed his sword.

Tiny giggled. "Here it comes!"

"Be quiet you damned necromancer! You—" Tulgord pointed his sword at Brash, whose poor visage was pallid as, well, Sellup's (above her mouth, that is). "You are sick—do you hear me? Sick!"

"Artists don't really view that as a flaw," observed Apto Canavalian.

The sword trembled. "No more," rasped Tulgord. "No more, do you hear me?"

Brash's head was bobbing like a turd in a whirlpool.

Done at last readying the horse I gave its dusty rump a pat and turned to Arpo Relent. "Your charger awaits you, sir."

"Excellent. Now what?"

"Well, you mount up."

"Good. Let's do that, then."

"Mounting up involves you walking over here, good knight."

"Right."

"Foot into the stirrup—no, the other—oh, never mind, that one will do. Now, grasp the back of the saddle, right, just so. And pull yourself up, swing that leg, yes, perfect, set your foot in the other—got it. Well done, sir."

"Where's its head?"

"Behind you. Guarding your back, sir, just the way you like it."

"I do, do I? Of course I do. Excellent."

"Now, we just tie these reins to this mule's harness here—do you mind, Mister Must?"

"Not in the least, Flicker."

"Good . . . there! You're set, sir."

"Most kind of you. Bless you, and take my blessing with solemn gratitude, mortal, it's been a thousand years since my last one."

"Then I shall, sir."

"For that," Tulgord said to me, "it's all down to you for the rest of the day, Flicker."

"Oh Mortal Sword, it is that indeed."

I would at this moment assert, humbly, that I am not particularly evil. In fact, if I was as evil as you perhaps think, why, I would have killed the critic long ago. We must bow, in either case, to the events as they truly transpired, though it might well paint me in modestly unpleasant hues. But the artist's eye must remain sharp and unforgiving, and every scene's noted detail must purport a burden of significance (something the least capable of critics never quite get into their chamber-potted brains, ah, piss on them I say!). The timing of this notification is, of course, entirely random and no doubt bred and born of my inherent clumsiness.

Leapt past that passage? Good for you. (And I do so look forward to your collected letters of erudition, posteritally)

"Just like the dog, tally ho!" shouted Arpo Relent as the journey resumed, and then arose a milked joccling sound followed by an audible shudder and visible moan from the Very Well Knight.

We set out, in the scuff of worn boots, the clop of hoofs and the rackle of carriage wheels, leaving in our wake Nifty Gum's corpse and Sellup who was now gnawing beneath the dead man's chin, in the works a love-bite of appalling proportions.

Shall I list we who remained? Why not. In the lead Steck Marynd, behind him Tulgord Vise and then the Chanters, followed by the host and Purse Snippet, then myself flanked by Apto upon my right and Brash upon my left, and behind us of course Mister Must and the carriage of the Dantoc Calmpositis, with Arpo Relent riding his mount off to one side at the trail's very edge.

Pilgrims one and all, and the day was bright, the vultures cooing and the bees writhing in the dust as the sun lit the landscape on fire and sweat ran in dirty streams to sting eyes and consciences both. Brash was gibbering under his breath, his gaze focused ten thousand paces ahead. Apto's mouth was also moving, perhaps taking mental notes or setting Brash's latest song to memory. Relish punched one of her brothers every now and then, with no obvious cause. Usually in the side of the head. Which the brothers endured with impressive indulgence, she being their little sister. Purse walked in a drugged daze which would not ebb until mid-morning, and bearing this in mind I pondered which of two tales would prove most timely at the moment, and, a decision having been reached with modest effort, I began to speak.

"The Imass woman, maiden no longer, awoke in the depths of night, in the time of the watch, which stretches cold and forlorn before the first touch of false dawn mocks the eastern sky. Shivering, she saw that her furs had been pulled aside, and of her lover no sign remained. Drawing the skins close, she drank the bitter air and with each deep breath her sleepiness grew more distant, and around her the hut breathed in its own dark pace, sighing its soot to settle upon her open eyes.

"She felt filled up, her skin tight as if someone had stuffed her as one would a carcass, to better stretch the curing hide. Her body was not quite entirely her own. She could feel the truth of this. Its privacy now a temporary condition, quick to surrender to his next touch. She was content with that, as only a young woman can be, for they are at their most generous at tender age, and it is only in the later years that the expanse contracts and borders are jealously guarded—trails carelessly trampled are by this time thoroughly mapped in her memory, after all.

"But now, this night, she is young still, and all of the world beyond this silent and unlit hut is blanketed in untouched snow, plush as a brold's virgin fur. The time of night known as the watch is a sacred time for many, and one of great and solemn responsibility. Malign spirits are known to stir in the breaths of the sleeping, seeking a way in, and so one of the tribe must be awake in vigil, whispering wards against the swollen darkness and its many-eyed hungers.

"She could hear nothing past her steady breathing, except perhaps something in the distance, out across the bold sweep of snow and frozen ground—the soft crackle from among trees, as frost tinkled down beneath black branches. There was no wind, and somehow she could feel the pressure of the stars, as if their glittering spears could reach through the layered hides of the hut's banked roof. And she told herself that the ancestors were protecting her with their unwavering regard, and with this thought she closed her eyes once more—"

I paused a moment, and then continued. "But then she heard

a sound. A faint scrape, the patter of droplets. She gasped. 'Beloved?' she whispered and spirits fled in the gloom. The hut's flap was drawn to one side, and the Fenn, crouched low to clear the doorway, edged inside. His eyes glistened as he paused.

"'Yes,' said he, 'It is I,' and then he made a soft sound, something like a laugh, she thought, though she could not be certain for it left a bitter trail. 'I have brought meat.' And at that she sat up. 'You hunted for us?' And in answer he drew closer and now she could smell charred flesh and she saw the thick strip bridging his hands. 'A gift,' he said, 'for the warmth you gave me, when I needed it most. I shall not forget you, not ever.' He presented her with the slab and she gasped again when it settled into her hands, for it was still hot, edges crisped by fire, and the fat streamed down between her fingers. Even so, something in what he had said troubled her and she felt a tightness in her throat as she said, 'Why would you forget me, beloved? I am here and so are you, and with this food we shall all bless you and beg that you remain with us, and then we—'

"'Hush,' said he. 'It cannot be. I must leave with the dawn. I must hold to the belief that among the tribes of the Fenn, those beyond the passes, I will find for myself a new home.'

"And now there were tears in her eyes and this he must have seen for he then said, 'Please, eat, gain strength. I beg you.' And she found the strength to ask, 'Will you sit with me when I eat? For this long at least? Will you—'"

"That's it?" demanded Relish. "She gave up that easily? I don't believe it."

"Her words were brave," I replied, "even as anguish tore at her heart."

"Well, how was I to know that?"

"By crawling into her skin, Relish," I said most gently. "Such is the secret covenant of all stories, and songs and poems too, for that matter. With our words we wear ten thousand skins, and with our words we invite you to do the same. We do not ask for your calculation, nor your cynicism. We do not ask you how well we are doing. You either choose to be with us, word by word, in and out of each and every scene, to breathe as we breathe, to walk as we walk, but above all, Relish, we invite that you *feel* as we feel."

"Unless you secretly feel nothing," Purse Snippet said, glancing back at me and I saw dreadful accusation in her eyes—her numbness had been burnt away, making my time short indeed.

"Is this what you fear? That my invitation is a deceit? The suspicion alone belongs to a cynic, to be sure—"

"Belongs to the wounded and the scarred, I should think," said Apto Canavalian. "Or the one whose own faith is dead."

"In such," said I, "no covenant is possible. Perhaps some artists do not feel what they ask others to feel, sir, but I do not count myself among those shameful and shameless wretches."

"I see that well enough," Apto said, nodding.

"Get back to the tale," demanded Tiny Chanter. "She asks him to stay while she eats. Does he?"

"He does," I replied, my eyes on Lady Snippet's back as she strode ahead of me. "The darkness of the hut was such that she could see little more than the glint of his eyes as he watched her, and in those twin flickers she imagined all manner of things. His love for her. His grief for all that he had lost. His pride in the food he had provided, his pleasure in her own as she bit into and savored the delicious meat. She believed she saw amusement as well, and she smiled in return, but slowly her smile faded, for the glitter now seemed too cold for humour, or perhaps it was something she was not meant to see.

"When she had at last finished and was licking the grease from her fingers, he reached out and settled a hand upon her belly. 'Two gifts,' murmured he, 'as you shall discover. Two.'"

"How did he know?" demanded Relish.

"Know what?" asked Brash Phluster.

"That she was pregnant, Relish? He knew and so too did she, for there was a new voice inside her, deep and soft, the tinkle of frost in a windless night."

"What then?" demanded Tiny.

"A moment, if you please. Purse Snippet, may I spin you a few lines of my tale for you?"

She looked back at me, frowning. "Now?"

"Yes, Lady, now."

She nodded.

"The brothers were very quick to act, and before a breath was let loose from their glowing sister, why, the man she had loved the night before was lying dead. In her soul a ragged wind whipped up a swirl of ashes and cinders, and she almost stumbled, and the tiny voice inside her—so precious, so new— now wailed piteously for the father it had lost so cruelly—"

Tiny bellowed and spun to Relish, who shrank back.

"Hold!" I cried, and an array of sibling faces swung snarling my way. "Beneath that tiny cry she found a sudden fury rising within her. And she vowed that when her child was born she would tell it the truth. She would again and again jab a sharp-nailed finger at her passing brothers and say to her sweet wide-eyed boy or girl: 'There! There is one of the men who murdered your father! Your vile, despicable, treacherous uncles! Do you see them! They sought to protect me—so they said, but they failed, and what did they then do, my child? *They killed your father!*' No, there would be no smiling uncles for that lone child, no tossing upon the saddle of a thigh, no squeals, no indulgent spoiling, no afternoons at the fishing hole, or wrestling bears or spitting boars with sticks. That child would know only hatred for those uncles, and a vow would find shape deep within it, a kin-slaying vow, a family-destroying vow. Blood in the future. Blood!"

All had halted. All were staring at me.

"She would," I continued with a voice of gravel and sharp stones. "She . . . *could.* If they would not leave her be. If they dogged her day after day. Her virginity was now gone. They had nothing left in her to protect. Unless, perhaps . . . an innocent child. But even then—she would decide when and how much. She was now in charge, not them. She was, and this was the sudden, blinding truth that seared through her mind at that instant: she was *free.*"

And then I fell silent.

Tiny gaped, at me and then at Relish. "But you said Callap—"

"I lied," replied Relish, crossing her arms and happily proving that she was not as witless as I had first imagined.

"But then you're not—"

"No, I'm not."

"And you're—"

"I am."

"The voice—"

"Yes."

"And you'll tell it—"

"If you leave me to live my life? Nothing."

"But—"

Her eyes flashed and she advanced on him. *"Everything.* The truth! Hate's seed—to become a mighty tree of death! Your death, Tiny! And yours, Midge! And yours, Flea!"

Tiny stepped back.

Midge stepped back.

Flea stepped back.

"Are we understood?" demanded Relish.

Three mute nods.

She whirled then and shot me a look of eternal gratitude or eternal resentment—I couldn't tell which and really, did it matter?

Did I then catch a wondering smile from Purse Snippet? I cannot be certain, for she quickly turned away.

As we resumed our journey Apto snorted under his breath. "Flick goes the first knife this day. Well done, oh, very well done."

The first. Yes, but only the first.

A voice from back down the trail made us turn. "Look everybody! I brought Nifty's head!"

There is a deftness that comes of desperation, but having never experienced desperation, I know nothing of it. The same woeful ignorance on my part can be said for the savage wall that rises like a curse between an artist and inspiration, or the torture of sudden doubt that can see scrolls heaped on the fire. The arrow of my intent is well trued. It sings unerringly to its target, even when that target lies beyond the horizon's swollen-breasted curve. You do not believe me? Too bad.

I imagine such flaws in my character are unusual, perhaps even rare enough to warrant a ponder or two, but to be honest, I can't be bothered, and if I must shoulder through jostling crowds of skepticism, suspicion and outright disbelief, then 'ware my spiked armour, for my path is ever sure and I will not be turned aside. Even when it takes me off the cliff's edge, I shall spare you all one last knowing nod. As is only fair.

Is this to also claim that I have lived a life without error? Ah, but recall the beginning of this tale, and find therein my answer to that. Errors salt the earth and patched, sodden and tangled is my garden, dear friends, riotous in mischance at every crook and bend. This being said, I find my confidence unsullied nonetheless, and indeed so replete my aplomb that one cannot help but see in the wild swirling cloak of my wake the sparkle and shock of my assured stride. Nary a tremulous step, do you see?

Not yet? Then bear witness, if you will, to the harrowed closing of this most truthful tale.

"I can't see where we're going. Someone make this horse walk backwards. A new decree, where are the priests? Those purple-lipped perverts fiddling under their robes—oh, damn me! Now I know what they were up to!"

Once more we walked Cracked Pot Trail, and somewhere in the distance awaited the Great Descent to the river and its ferry landing. By day's close, or so our increasingly agitated host had proclaimed. An end to this nightmare—the fevered hope was bright in Brash Phluster's eyes, and even Apto Canavalian's stride was a stitch quicker.

Still the heat tormented. Our water was almost gone, the pieces of Callap Roud bubbling in our bellies, and our dastardly deeds clung to our shoulders with talon and fang. It did not help that Sellup was scooping out handfuls of Nifty's brain and making yummy sounds as she slopped the goo into her mouth.

Tulgord Vise, glancing back and taking note of this detail, twisted round to glare at Tiny Chanter. "By the Blessed Mounds, do something about her or I will."

"No. She's growing on me, isn't she, Flea?"

"She is. Midge?"

"She—"

"Stop that too!"

The three brothers laughed, and Relish did, as well, stirring in me a few curdles of unease, especially the way she now walked, bold, swaggering the way curvy women did, her head held high and all those black tresses drifting around like ghostly serpents with glinting tongues testing the air. Why, I realized with a start, she really thought she was pregnant. All the signs were there.

Now, as any mother would tell you, pregnancy and freedom do not belong in the same sentence, except one indicating the loss of the latter with the closing pangs of the former. That being said, I'm no mother, nor was I in any way inclined to disavow

Relish Chanter of whatever comforting notions she happened to hold at the time, and was this not considerate of me?

"Look at me! I'm Nifty Gum the famous poet!" Sellup had jammed her hand up inside the head and was moving the jaw up and down, making the teeth clack. "I say poet things! All the time! I have a new poem for everybody. Want to hear? It's called The Lay of the Eggs! Ha ha, get it? A poem about eggs! I'm famous and everything and my brains taste like cheese!"

"Stop that," Tulgord Vise said in a dangerous growl, one hand finding the grip of his sword.

"I have found ruts," announced Steck Marynd from up ahead, reining in and leaning hard over his saddle as he squinted at the ground. "Carriage ruts, and heavy ones too."

Tulgord rode up. "How long ago?" he demanded.

"A day, maybe less!"

"We'll catch them at the ferry! At last!"

"Could be any carriage, couldn't it?" so queried Apto Canavalian, earning vicious stares from Tulgord and the Chanter brothers. "I mean," he stumbled on, "might not be those Nehemoth at all, right? Another pilgrim train, or—"

"Aye," admitted Steck. "Worth keeping in mind, and we're worn out, we are. Worn out. We can push, but not too hard." He tilted his crossbow towards Sardic Thew. "You, tell us about this ferry. How often does it embark? How long the crossing?"

Our host rubbed his lean jaw. "Once a day, usually at dusk. There's a tidal draw, you see, that it needs to ride across to Farrog. Reaches the docks by dawn."

"Dusk?" Steck's narrow eyes narrowed some more. "Can we make it, Thew?"

"With a decent pace and no halt for lunch . . . yes, woodsman, I would say it is possible."

The air fairly bristled, and savage the smiles of Tiny, Midge, Flea and Tulgord Vise.

"What is all this?" demanded Arpo Relent, kicking his horse round so that he could see the rest of the party. "Are we chasing someone, then? What is he, a demon? I despise demons. If we catch him I'll cut him to pieces. Pieces. Proclamation! The Guild of Demons is herewith disbanded, with prejudice! What, who set the city on fire? Well, put it out! Doesn't this temple have any windows? I can't see a damned thing through all this smoke—someone kill a priest. That always cheers me up. Ho, what's this?"

"Your penis," said Apto Canavalian. "And before anyone asks, no, I have no particular fascination for that word."

"But what's it do? Oh, now I remember. Hmmm, nice."

"We pursue not a demon," said Tulgord Vise, straightening to assume a virtuous pose in knightly fashion. "Necromancers of the worst sort. Evil, murderous. We have avowed that in the name of goodness they must die."

Arpo blinked up from his blurred right hand. "Necromancers? Oh, them. Miserable fumblers, don't know a damned thing, really. Well, I'm happy to obliterate them just the same. Did someone mention Farrog? I once lived in a city called Fan'arrogal, wonder if it's, uh, related. On a river mouth? Crawling with demons? Ooh, see that? Ooh! New building program. Fountains!"

You will be relieved that I bit off a comment about pubic works.

Tulgord stared wide-eyed at Arpo, which was understandable, and then he tugged his horse back onto the path. "Lead us on, Marynd. I want this done with."

Mister Must then spoke from atop the carriage. "Fan'arrogal, you said?"

Arpo was wiping his hand on his bared chest. "My city. Until the demon infestation, when I got fed up with the whole thing." He frowned, gaze clouding. "I think."

"After a night of slaughter that left most of the city in smouldering ruins," Mister Must said, his eyes thinned to slits behind his pipe's smoke. "Or so the tale went. Farrog rose up from its ashes."

"Gods below," whispered Sardic Thew with eyes bulging upon Arpo Relent, "you're the Indifferent God! Returned to us at last!"

Brash Phluster snorted. "He's a man with a cracked skull, Thew. Look what's leaking out now, will you?"

"I'd rather not," said Apto, quickly setting off after the Nehemothanai.

I regarded Mister Must. "Fan'arrogal? That name appears in only the obscurest histories of the region."

Wiry brows lifted. "Indeed now? Well, had to have picked it up somewhere, didn't I?"

"As footmen will do," said I, nodding.

Grunting, Mister Must snapped the traces and the mules lurched forward. I stepped to one side and found myself momentarily alone, as the others had already hurried after the Nehemothanai. Well, almost alone.

"I'm Nifty Gum and I'll do anything she says!" *Clack-clack.*
Ah, a fan's dream, what?

"Kill some time," commanded Tiny Chanter, once I had
caught up.

"Her tears spilled down upon the furs when, with a final soft
caress, he left the hut. The grey of dawn mocked all the colours
in the world, and in this lifeless realm she sat unmoving, as a
faint wind moaned awake outside. Earlier, she had listened for
the sled's runners scraping the snow, but had heard nothing.
Now, she listened for the bickering among the hunting dogs,
the crunch of wrapped feet as the ice over the pits was cracked
open. She listened for the cries of delight upon finding the carcass of the animal the Fenn had slain.

"She listened, then, for the sounds of her life of yesterday
and all the days before it, for as long as she could remember.
The sounds of childhood, which in detail did not change
though she was a child no longer. He was gone, a cavern carved
out of her soul. He had brought dark words and bright gifts, in
the way of strangers and unexpected guests.

"But, beyond this hut . . . only silence."

"A vicious tale," commented Steck Marynd. "You should have
let it die with Roud."

"The demand was otherwise," I replied to the man riding a
few strides ahead. "In any case, the end, as you well know, is
now near. Finally, she rose, heavy and weightless, chilled and

almost fevered, and with her furs drawn about her she emerged into the morning light.

"Dead dogs were strewn about on the stained snow, their necks snapped. To the left of the Chief's hut the remnants of a bonfire died in a drift of ashes and bones. The corpses of her beloved kin were stacked in frozen postures of cruel murder beside the ghastly hearth, and closer to hand laid the butchered remnants of three children.

"The sled with its mute cargo remained where he had left it, although the hides had been taken, exposing the frost-blackened body of another Fenn. Dead of a sword thrust.

"A keening cry lifting up through the numbness of her soul, she staggered closer to that sled, and she looked down upon a face years younger than that of the Fenn who had come among them. For, as is known to all, age is difficult to determine among the Tartheno Toblakai. She then recalled his tale, the battle upon the glacier, and all at once she understood—"

"What?" demanded Midge. "Understood what? Hood take you, Flicker, explain!"

"It is the hero who wins the fated battle against his evil enemy," said I, with unfeigned sorrow. "So it is in all tales of comfort. But there is no comfort in this tale. Alas, while we may rail, sometimes the hero dies. Fails. Sometimes, the last one standing is the enemy, the Betrayer, the Kinslayer. Sometimes, dear Midge, there is no comfort. None."

Apto Canavalian fixed upon me an almost accusatory glare. "And what," he said, voice rough with fury, "is the moral of that story, Flicker?"

"Moral? Perhaps none, sir. Perhaps, instead, the tale holds another purpose."

"Such as?"

Purse Snippet answered in the coldest of tones. "A warning."

"A warning?"

"Where hides the gravest threat? Why, the one you invite into your camp. Avas Didion Flicker, you should have abandoned this tale—gods, what was Roud thinking?"

"It was the only story he knew by heart!" Brash Phluster snapped, and then he wheeled on me. "But you! You know plenty! You could have spun us a different one! Instead—instead—"

"He chooses to sicken our hearts," Purse said. "I said I would abide, Flicker. For a time. Your time, I think, has just run out."

"The journey has not ended yet, Lady Snippet. If firm you will hold to this bargain, then I have the right to do the same."

"Do you imagine I remain confident of your prowess?"

I met her eyes, my lockbox of secrets cracked open—just a sliver—but enough to steal the colour from her face, and I said this, "You should be by now, Lady."

How many worlds exist? Can we imagine places like and yet unlike our own? Can we see the crowds, the swarming sea of strangers and all those faces scratching our memories, as if we once knew them, even when we knew them not? What value building bitter walls between us? After all, is it not a conceit to shake one's head in denial of such possibilities, when in our very own world we can find a multitude of worlds, one behind the eyes of every man, woman, child and beast you happen to meet?

Or would you claim that these are in fact all facets of the same world? A man kneels in awe before a statue or standing stone, whilst another pisses at its base. Do these two men see the same thing? Do they even live in the same world?

And if I tell you that I have witnessed each in turn, that indeed I have both bowed in humility and reeled before witless desecration, what value my veracity when I state with fierce certainty that numberless worlds exist, and are in eternal collision, and that the only miracle worth a damned thing is that we manage to agree on *anything*?

Nothing stinks worse than someone else's piss. And if you do not believe me, friends, try standing in my boots for a time.

And so to this day I look with fond indulgence upon my memories of the Indifferent God, if god he was, there within the cracked pot of Arpo Relent's head, for all the pure pleasure he found in the grip of his right hand. Its issue was one of joy, after all, and far preferable to the spiteful, small-minded alternative.

The name of Avas Didion Flicker is not entirely unknown among the purveyors of entertainment, if not culture, throughout Seven Cities, and by virtue of living as long as I have, I am regarded with some modest veneration. This has not yielded vast wealth, not by any measure beyond that of personal satisfaction at the canon of words marking a lifetime's effort, and as everyone knows, satisfaction is a wavering measure in one's own mind, as quick to pale as it is to glow. If I now choose to stand full behind this faint canon and its even fainter reputation, well, the stance is not precisely comfortable.

And the relevance of this humble admission? Well now, that's the question, isn't it?

Mortal Sword Tulgord Vise had girthed himself for battle. Weapons cluttered his scaled hands, the pearled luminescence of his armour was fair blinding in the noble light. His eyes were savage arrow-heads straining at the taut bowstring of righteous anticipation. His beard bristled like the hackled rump of a furious hedgehog. The veins webbing his nose were bursting into crimson blooms beneath the skin. His teeth gnashed with every flare of his nostrils and strange smells swirled in his wake.

The Chanter brothers walked in a three-man shieldwall, suddenly festooned with halberds and axes and two-handed and even three-handed swords. Swathed in bear skin, Tiny commanded the centre, with the seal skinned Midge on his left and the seal skinned Flea on his right, thus forming a bestial wall in need of a good wash. Relish sauntered a step behind them, regal as a pregnant queen immune to bastardly rumours (they're just jealous).

Steck Marynd still rode ahead, crossbow at the ready. Two thousand paces ahead the trail lifted to form a rumpled ridge, and behind it was naught but sky. Flanking this ominously near horizon was a host of crooked, leaning standards from which depended sun-bleached rags flapping like the wings of skewered birds. Every dozen or so heartbeats Steck twisted round in his saddle to look upon the Chanters, who being on foot were dictating the pace of this avenging army. He visibly ground his teeth at their insouciance.

Purse Snippet, with visage fraught and drawn, cast pensive glances my way, as did Sardic Thew and indeed Apto Canavalian, but still I held my silence. Yes, I could feel the twisting, knotting strain of the Nehemothanai, possibly only moments from launching forward, but I well knew that neither Tulgord nor Steck were such fools as to abandon the alliance with the Chanters upon the very threshold of battle. By all counts, Bauchelain and Korbal Broach were deadly, both in sorcery and in hard iron. Indeed, if but a small portion of the tales we had all heard on this pilgrimage were accurate, why, the necromancers had left a trail of devastation across half the known world, and entire frothing armies now nipped at their heels.

No, the Chanters, formidable and vicious, would be needed. And what of Arpo Relent? Why, he could be host to a terrible god, and had he not promised assistance?

Yet, for all this, the very air creaked.

"Gods," whispered Brash Phluster clawing at his hair, "let them find them! I cannot bear this!"

I fixed my placid gaze upon the broad furry back of Tiny Chanter. "Perhaps the enemy is closer than any might imagine." So I spoke, at a pitch that might or might not reach that lumbering shieldwall. "After all, what secrets did Calap Roud possess? Did he not choose his tale after much consideration? Or so I seem to recall."

Apto frowned. "I don't—"

Tiny Chanter swung round, weapons shivering. "You! Flicker!"

"Lady Snippet," said I, calm as ever, "There is more to my tale, my gift to you, this offering of redemption in this sullied, terrible world."

Tulgord barked something to Steck who reined in and then wheeled his mount. The entire party had now halted, Mister Must grunting in irritation as he tugged on his traces.

Arpo looked round. "Is it raining again? Bouncing cat eyes, how I hate rain!"

"Through gritted teeth and clenched jaws," I began, eyes fixed upon Purse Snippet's, "do we not despair of the injustice that plagues our precious civilization? Are we not flayed by the unfairness to which we are ever witness? The venal escape unscathed. The corrupt duck into shadows and leave echoes of mocking laughter. Murderers walk the streets. Bullies grow hulking and make fortunes buying and selling property. Legions of black-tongued clerks steal from you every last coin, whilst their shrouded masters build extensions to their well-guarded vaults. Money lenders recline in the filth of riches stripped from the poor. Justice? How can one believe in justice when it bleeds and crawls, when it wears a thousand faces and each one dying before your very eyes? And without justice, how can redemption survive? We are whipped round, made to turn our backs on notions of righteous restitution, and should we raise our voices in protest, why, our heads are lopped off and set on spikes as warnings to everyone else. 'Keep in line, you miserable shits, or you'll end up like this!'"

Now that I had their attention, even Nifty's, I waved my arms about, consumed by pious wrath. "Shall we plead to the gods for justice?" And I jabbed a finger at Arpo Relent. "Do so, then!

One is among us! But be warned, justice cuts clean, and what you ask for could well slice you in two on the backswing!" I wheeled to face Purse Snippet once again. "Do you believe in justice, Lady?"

Mutely she shook her head.

"Because you have seen! With your own eyes!"

"Yes," she whispered. "I have seen."

I hugged myself, wretched with all my haunting thoughts. "Evil hides. Sometimes right in front of you. I hear something . . . something. It's close. Yes, close. Lady, to our tale, then. She walked in the company of pilgrims and killers, but as the journey went on, as the straits grew ever direr, she began to lose the distinction—there among her companions, even within her own soul. Which the pilgrim? Which the killer? The very titles blurred in blood-stained mockery—how could she remain blind to that? How could anyone?

"And so, as dreadful precipices loomed ever closer, it seemed the world was swallowed in grisly confusion. Killers, yes, on all sides. Wearing brazen faces. Wearing veiled ones. The masks all hide the same bloodless visage, do they not? Where is the enemy? Where? Somewhere ahead, just beyond the horizon? Or somewhere much closer. What was that warning again? Ah, yes . . . be careful who you invite into your camp. I hear something. What is it? Is it laughter? I think—"

Bellowing, Tiny Chanter pushed through our ranks and thumped against the carriage. "Everyone quiet!" And he set the side of his head against the shuttered side window. "I hear . . . *breathing.*"

"Yes," said Mister Must, looking down, "she does that."

"No! It's—it's—"

"'Ware off there, sir," rumbled Mister Must, his stained teeth visible where they clenched the clay stem of his pipe. "I am warning you. Back off . . . now."

"An old woman, is it?" Tiny sneered up at the driver. "Eats enough to shame a damned wolf!"

"Her appetites are her business—"

Steck kicked his horse closer. "Flicker—"

"By my bloody altar!" cried Arpo Relent, "I just noticed!"

Tulgord raised his sword, head whipping round. "What? What did you just—"

The pipe stem snapped between Mister Must's teeth and he set most narrow eyes upon the Well Knight. "Let the past lie, I always say. Deep in the quiet earth, deep and—"

"I know you!" Arpo roared, and then he launched himself at Mister Must.

Something erupted, engulfing the driver in flames. Arms outstretched, Arpo plunged into that raging maelstrom. Braying, the mules lunged forward.

Tiny flung himself onto the side of the carriage, hammering at the door. An instant later Flea and Midge joined him, clambering like wild apes. Where Mister Must had been there was now a demon, monstrous, locked in a deathgrip with Arpo Relent, as flames writhed like serpents around them both.

The carriage heaved forward as the mules strained in their harnesses.

Everyone scattered from its careening path.

Tulgord Vise fought with his rearing charger, and the beast twisted, seeking to evade the mules, Arpo's tethered horse and the crowded carriage, only to collide with Steck Marynd's shaggy mare.

The crossbow loosed, the quarrel burying itself in the rump of Tulgord's mount. Squealing, the beast lunged, shot forward, colliding with Steck's horse. That creature went down, rolling over Steck Marynd and loud was the snap of one of the woodsman's legs. Tulgord had lost grip on his reins, and now tottered perilously as his horse charged up alongside the carriage.

More flames ignited, bathing the front half of the rollicking, thundering conveyance.

Tulgord's mount veered suddenly, throwing the Mortal Sword from the saddle, and down he went, rolling once before the front left wheel ground over him in a frenzied crunching of enameled armour, followed by the rear wheel, and then his weapon belt went taut in a snapping of leather, and off the man went, dragged in the carriage's wake, and in spinning, curling clouds of smoke, the whole mess thundered ahead, straight for the edge of the Great Descent.

Steck Marynd was screaming in agony as his horse staggered upright once more, and the beast set off in mindless pursuit of the carriage, Tulgord's mount and Arpo's falling in alongside it. Relish howled and ran after them, her hair flying out to surround her head in black fronds.

Mute, we followed, stumbling, staggering.

None could miss the moment when the mad mob plunged over the crest and vanished from sight. It is an instant of appalling clarity, seared into my memory. And we saw, too, when the horses did the same, and through drifting smoke and clouds of dust we were witness to Relish Chanter finally arriving, skidding to a halt, and her horrified cry was so curdling Nifty's head went rolling across our paths as Sellup clapped greasy hands to her rotting earholes. Relish set off down the slope and we could see her no more.

There are instances in life when no cogent thought is possible. When even words vanish and nothing rises to challenge a choke-tight throat, and each breath is a shocked torment, and all one's limbs move of their own accord, loose as a drunkard's, and a numbness spreads from a gaping mouth. And on all sides, the world is suddenly painfully sharp. Details cut and rend the eyes. The sheer brilliant stupidity of stones and dead grasses and clouds and twigs strewn like grey bones on the path—all this, then, strike the eye like mailed fists. Yes, there are instances in life when all this assails a person.

It was there in the face of Apto Canavalian. And in Purse Snippet's, and even in Brash Phluster's (behind the manic joy of his impending salvation). Sardic Thew's oily hands were up at his oily lips, his eyes glittering and he led us all in the rush to the trail's edge.

At last we arrived, and looked down.

The carriage had not well survived the plunge, its smashed wreckage heaped in the midst of flames and smoke at the distant base, three hundred steep strides down the rocky, treacherous path. Bits of it were scattered about here and there, flames licking or smoke twirling. Astonishingly, the mules had somehow escaped their harnesses and were swimming out into the twisting streams of the vast river that stretched out from a cluster of shacks and a stone jetty at the ferry's landing. Immediately behind them bobbed the heads of three horses.

Of the demon and Arpo Relent, there was no sign, but we could see Flea's body lying among boulders just this side of the muddy bank, and Midge's bloody form was sprawled flat on its face two-thirds of the way down the track. Tiny, however, seemed to have vanished, perhaps inside the burning wreckage, and perhaps the same fate had taken Tulgord Vise, for he too was nowhere to be seen.

Skidding and stumbling, Relish had almost reached Midge.

And the ferry?

Fifty or more reaches out on the river, a large, flat-decked thing, on which stood four horses, and a tall carriage, black and ornate as a funeral bier. Figures standing at the stern rail were visible.

Sardic Thew, our most venerable host, was staring intently down at the burning carriage. He licked his lips. "Is she—is she?"

"Dead?" asked I. "Oh yes, indeed."

"You are certain?"

I nodded.

He wiped at his face, and then reached a trembling hand

beneath his robes and withdrew a silk bag that jingled most fetchingly. He settled its substantial weight into my palm.

I dipped my head in thanks, hid the fee beneath my cloak and then walked a half-dozen paces away to settle my gaze on that distant ferry.

Behind me a conversation began.

"Gods below!" hissed Apto Canavalian. "The Dantoc—an old woman—"

"A vicious beast, you mean," growled Sardic Thew. "Relations of mine got into financial trouble. Before I could assume the debts, that slavering bitch pounced. It was the daughter she wanted, you see. For her pleasure pits. Just a child! A sweet, innocent—"

"Enough!" I commanded, wheeling round. "Your reasons are you own, sir. You have said more than I need hear, do you understand?" And then I softened my eyes and fixed them upon a pale, trembling Purse Snippet. "So few, Lady, dare believe in justice. Ask our host, if you must hear more of this sordid thing. For me, and understand this well, I am what I am, no more and no less. Do I sleep at night? Most serenely, Lady. Yes, I see what there is in your eyes when you look upon me. Does redemption await me? I think not, but who can truly say, till the moment of its arrival. If you seek some softness in your self-regard, find it by measure against the man who stands before you now. And should you still find nothing of worth within you, then you can indeed have my life."

After a time, she shook her head. That, and nothing more.

Sellup arrived. "Anybody see Nifty's head? I lost it. Anyone?"

. . .

"Do you believe that art possesses relevance in the real world?"
"Now, that is indeed a difficult question. After all, whose art?"
To that I shrugged. "Pray, don't ask me."

Knives, garrotes, poison, so very crass. Oh, in my long and sto-ried career, I have made use of them all as befits my profession, but I tell you this. Nothing is sweeter than murder by word, and that sweetness, dear friends, remains as fresh today as it did all those many years ago, on that dusty ridge that marked the end of Cracked Pot Trail.

Did I receive my reward from Purse Snippet? Why, on the night of the tumultuous party upon the awarding of the Cen-tury's Greatest Artist to Brash Phluster (such a bright, rising star!), she did find me upon a private island amidst the swirl of smiling humanity, and we spoke then, at surprising length, and thereafter—

Oh dear, modesty being what it is, I can take that no further.

It was a considerable time afterwards (months, years?) that I happened to meet the grisly Nehemoth, quarry of ten thou-sand stone-eyed hunters, and over guarded cups of wine a few subjects were brushed, dusted off here and there in the gentle and, admittedly, cautious making of acquaintances. But even without that most intriguing night, it should by now be well understood that the true poet can never leave a tale's threads woefully unknotted. Knotting the tale's end is a necessity, to be sure, isn't it? Or, rather if not entirely knotted, then at least seared, with finger tips set to wet mouth. To cut the sting.

So, with dawn nudging the drowsing birds in this lush garden, the wives stirring from their nests and the moths dipping under leaf, permit me to wing us back to that time, and to one last tale, mercifully brief, I do assure you.

Thus.

"It is a true measure of civilization's suicidal haste," said Bauchelain, "that even a paltry delay of, what? A day? Two? Even that, Mister Reese, proves so unpalatable to its hapless slaves, that death itself is preferable." And he gestured with gloved hand towards all that the passing of the dust cloud now revealed upon that distant shore.

Emancipor Reese puffed for a time on his pipe, and then he shook his head. "Couldn't they see, Master? That is what I can't get. Here we were, and it's not like that old ferryman there was gonna turn us round, is it? They missed the ride and that's that. It baffles me, sir, that it does."

Bauchelain stroked his beard. "And still you wonder at my haunting need to, shall we say, *adjust* the vicissitudes of civilization as befits its more reasonable members? Just so." He was quiet for a time until he cleared his throat and said, "Korbal Broach tells me that the city we shall see on the morn groans beneath the weight of an indifferent god, and I do admit we have given that some thought."

"Oh? Well, Master," said Emancipor, leaning on the rail,

"better an indifferent one than the opposite, wouldn't you say?"

"I disagree. A god that chooses indifference in the face of its worshippers has, to my mind, Mister Reese, reneged on the most precious covenant of all. Accordingly, Korbal and I have concluded that its life is forfeit."

Emancipor coughed out a lungful of smoke.

"Mister Reese?"

"Sorry!" gasped the manservant, "but I thought you just said you mean to kill a god!"

"Indeed I did, Mister Reese. Heavens forbid, it's not like there's a shortage of the damned things, is there? Now then, best get you some rest. The city awaits our footfalls upon the coming dawn and not even an unmindful god can change that now."

And we can all forgive their not hearing the muttering that came from the ferryman's dark hood as he hunched over the tiller, one hand fighting the currents, and the other beneath his breeches. *"That's what you think."*